The
Forester's
Tale

George Sousa
Tanya Sousa

Forestry Press, Inc.
www.forestrypress.com

Chapter One

It was early morning, the sun just peering over the horizon. Rays shone down upon an old forest, the plants still bathed by sparkling dew. The sun glowed through the foliage and created a cathedral of exotic greens, golds, and hints of red more splendid than any man-made stained glass.

A well-worn trail meandered through these great trees and came out through the morning mist. A figure appeared, moving from the cloak of white on the path into the lighted space of a slight clearing. The figure stopped for a moment and stretched even taller than he already was, his khaki clothing pulling up as he reached to the sky, higher still, and finally released the stretch with a relieved puff of breath. His face was weather worn, a hard plastic hat set upon salt and pepper curly hair. His eyes, like the foliage, were layers of color—sometimes seeming to be a light brown, other times more gray, and today, reflecting the forest around him, showing hints of green.

He stopped, picked up some fallen limbs that barred the path, and looked about, squinting with a critical gaze like a wise wood elf as he took silent note of the damage done from winter snows and spring rains. "All in all, not too bad," he announced in a soft, almost reverent voice. He smiled. This part of the trail was still in good shape; his work from last year had paid off. However, there were many miles of it to maintain, and there was plenty of work to be done over the summer—spots that hadn't fared so well. He reached for a handkerchief and mopped the moisture of cool dew from his face and neck and continued on his way. There was a spring in his step, and he began to whistle a tune that seemed to harmonize with the piping and tuning of the birds.

The forest became denser the farther he traveled. He stopped from time to time to drag away fallen branches. He knew he would need to come back with his chainsaw to clear away the larger trees that had crashed down, trees that had given way to some wind or other weather, but he never did that at the start of the season—never in the sanctity of the morning.

He worked silently except for the occasional whistling to free fleeting songs that entered his mind, his hands moving, his body moving, free of worry and thought except for his purpose at that moment.

It wasn't always how he'd been.

The Forester didn't need a watch to know when it was time for a break and lunch, but he would have to find a comfortable place to settle. His eyes fell on grand old maple trees with a small clearing among them; it would be a fine place to rest. He dropped his backpack to the ground after pulling out a sandwich, an apple, and a thermos of cold water. He used the pack for a seat, his back leaning against the strong trunk of one maple that had probably seen one hundred years or more of life.

He chewed slowly, his eyes moving here and there to see if he could find some movement on the forest floor. Before long, a smile played upon his lips, twitching at the corners as he tried to be completely still. A rabbit stood on its hind legs about thirty feet from him, ears turning and nose wiggling, taking him in and trying to label him friend or foe. Eventually, feeling no threat, the rabbit came down on all fours and hopped across the clearing and disappeared again into the thicker brush beyond.

The Forester finished his meal and rose. He continued on the path, working steadily and somehow easily for another hour before reaching a tremendous oak. He looked up at this grandfather of trees, and his eyes misted as he studied the old-timer that had died many years ago. Great limbs lay at its base, nourishing the new growth of saplings that had sprung from beneath the oak's still massive trunk. He slowly walked around it all, noticing that part of its girth had rotted out, making it a shelter for animals. Other parts had been hollowed purposefully by woodpeckers. God's cycle. Nature's cycle. Still, endings saddened him no matter how necessary. He drew in a suddenly jagged breath and laid his hand on the oak. "I will make it so people will stop here and see how great you were, and that in death you create new life." He pulled creased paper and a pencil out of his pack, deftly drawing plans for a bench that he would build of strewn limbs nearby. His plans took in mind the safety of the wildflowers that also grew close: trilliums and even a rare lady's slipper. He'd been meaning to do this for some time.

As The Forester left the woods behind for the day, he turned and looked back before facing the fields that once fed cattle. Now they were abandoned. Scraggly brush grew here and there, and piles of rocks sat in widely scattered mounds where farmers and their sons had picked stones from the land, placing them in these spots so the area could be grazed and hayed. In the distance a shed stood rotting; the barn and home had fallen in many years ago. The Forester adjusted his pack and headed down the old gravel road where he had parked his Rover.

He drove along, dodging holes and large rocks that had worked their way up from the ground. This road, like the field, had been unused for years except as a way for hikers to find their way to the trail.

He reached for the switch on his dash to turn on the headlights. No sooner had he done this than a large moose stepped into the road. He knew this moose, and he also knew she would take her sweet time. He put the Rover into park and took a small candy bar from the glove box, chewing slowly. "Don't hurry now, Bessy," he called out the window to her. She turned her large head his way. By the time he finished the candy bar, she began to move deliberately to the side of the road, at least leaving enough room so he could carefully pass.

Soon, he reached an old log cabin tucked away among the trees, and he pulled into a leaf-covered space that functioned as a driveway. The happy, raucous bark of his dog filled the air—a faithful companion for the last six years in this place. He opened the cabin door, and a ball of fur burst out in a delighted frenzy, all tail and tongue, until The Forester's lined face pulled tight with laughter. "Enough!" In reply, his friend sniffed the khaki pants, then the trail to the Rover, finally inspecting every inch of the Rover tires to discover at least part of The Forester's day. "I saw a rabbit," he told the dog, who sat down and tilted his head. "Oh, come on! It's time to eat and I've got to shower. Even your nose must agree with that."

Later, he took out an old worn Bible, caressing the cover automatically before opening to a random page. His eyes scanned the first words about King Nebuchadnezzar and his second dream. First, the king told Daniel of a vision of a huge tree that reached to the sky and could be seen by everyone in the world. He told of its beautiful leaves and its abundance of fruit enough for the whole world to eat, and how wild animals rested in its shade, birds built nests in its branches, and every living being ate its fruit. While pondering this vision, an angel came from heaven and said, *"Cut the tree down and chop off its branches. Strip it of its leaves and fruit. Drive away the animals from under it and the birds from its branches, but leave the stump in the ground with a band of iron and bronze around it."*

The Forester stopped reading. He stared mutely ahead. The dog raised his eyes to the man, but he wasn't really looking at the dog or anything in the cabin at all. The mirror of his mind saw the great oak with its fallen branches and leafless limbs that remained rotting beside its stump. For a moment, The Forester pictured it in all its glory like the tree in the king's dream. He stirred in his chair and read on.

The king continued telling his dream to Daniel. The angel had said, "Now let the dew fall on this man and let him live with the animals and the plants. For seven years he will not have a human mind, but the mind of an animal. This is the decision of the alert and watchful angels. So then, let all people everywhere know that the Supreme God has power over human kingdoms, and that he can give them to any he chooses—even to the least important of men."

The book fell to his lap, his hands rushing to his face, and he sobbed. He had instantly seen himself standing among the trees, ferns, and animals, tending them, wiping dew from his brow.

He hadn't always been that way. At one time, he had been a wealthy man with a successful business. He had a beautiful home surrounded by flower gardens tended by his wife. He could still see her humming and pruning, picking special blooms to put on the table. His two young daughters had played games in the yard and later pestered him for advice about boys who were never good enough for them. He had friends, a sense of importance, everything a man could want.

But then he'd lost the business during a hard recession. Not long after, his wife was diagnosed with a rare cancer. She went into her flower gardens less and less often, until finally she could only lay in bed waiting for the end. Their grown daughters brought her flowers that she would see and smile. The youngest brought lily of the valley, and the eldest wild roses. He had picked her forget-me-nots and brushed the blue petals against her cheek on her last day. Not that he had much left to lose, but the medical bills had stripped him of any savings he had left.

Afterwards, both daughters moved some distance away, and their own busy lives pulled them into new worlds of their own making. The people he thought were friends vaporized with the business and the fleeting wealth he'd enjoyed. One by one the things that had made his life rich left him, until the loneliness seemed to eat away at his soul.

His soul seemed to shatter the day the house was taken by the bank. A woman in a sharp tweed business suit walked up the stone steps, surrounded by his wife's flowerbeds, and changed the lock.

"Dad, you can come live with us until you get back on your feet," his eldest offered.

A shamed anger welled up inside. "I'm capable of taking care of myself. I built a business from nothing!"

So he unlocked a new door each day to a drab one-room apartment. He tried to cook, but couldn't seem to taste anything. He started looking for jobs, but after seeing younger men and women's eyes widen with a horrible pity that he wasn't the "right fit," he went out searching less and less. "You're too old" was what the eyes were really saying.

A knock came on his door one day, jolting him clumsily from sleep in the middle of the day. It was hard for him to focus on what the sound was, on what he should do about it. He didn't want to be awake. He didn't want to feel pain any more, but the knock continued and got louder and faster. A familiar voice called out his name, muffled from behind the wood: "Are you in there? Open the door."

A glimmer of recognition sparked his foggy mind, and he slowly shuffled to the door. It seemed so far away, but he reached it at last on shaky legs, and pulled it open to reveal a thin, short man with a usually smiling face now set with concern. "Friend," the man's voice lowered and softened. I'm bringing you home with me."

A chill in the room snapped The Forester out of his reverie, the tears starting to dry in the creases of his face. He rubbed his hands briskly over his eyes and cheeks and looked to the woodstove. The spring evenings were still cold enough that he needed it, and he must have been lost in his thoughts long enough that the embers had gotten low. "Hopefully not too low," he murmured. He rose, picked up a log from a small pile, and placed it on some still glowing coals. He blew, waited then blew again patiently until the flames licked at their new food as if savoring it. With a few well-placed pokes, the log finally roared into flame. Satisfied, he turned and walked to the bed, where he changed into flannel pants and laid back, pulling the soft sheet up and falling into a deep dreamless sleep.

Chapter Two

The next morning brought the weekend sun in a flood to the old wooden bed. It crept relentlessly in until it tapped the tan, rough skin of The Forester, first touching his cheek, then crossing his eyes in flickering flashes that caused him to stir and blink. He turned his face away to hide from the intruder, but his triumph was short-lived—the sun had found an ally. Hearing his master stir, the dog rose and approached his friend, licked his face and whined insistently in his ear. The meaning was clear enough without words: Hunger! Breakfast! Out!

The Forester reached his hand to ruffle the dog's fur before surrendering with a wide yawn. "Eggs this morning?" The dog thumped his tail and followed the man's morning shuffle to the door so he could go outside. The Forester mixed up some eggs in a frying pan with a bit of bacon, took half and mixed it with dry dog food in a silver bowl, and set it on the floor. He scraped his half on a simple white plate and grabbed a handful of grapes before going to the small corner table. He let his grateful dog in and sat down to eat as the dog made quick, clattering work of his own meal.

The Forester thoughtfully chewed grapes, popping them in his mouth slowly, one after another, and eyed the Bible on a small end table next to him. He pushed his empty plate away and took the book into his hands. He should finish the story he started last night. He carefully opened it to the page where he'd left off the night before, hesitating as the memory of his tears and pain were still fresh. Setting his mouth in a thin line, he continued.

Daniel, upon hearing this dream from the king, was so alarmed that he could not say anything. The king saw this and said, "Don't let the dream and message alarm you."

Daniel replied, "Your Majesty, I wish that the dream and its explanation applied to your enemies and not to you. The tree, so tall that it reached the sky, could be seen by everyone in the world. Your Majesty, you are the tree, tall and strong. You have grown so great that you reach the sky, and your power extends over the whole earth. While your Majesty was watching, an angel came down from heaven and said, 'Cut the tree down and destroy it, but leave the stump in the ground.' This, then, is what it means, your Majesty, and this is what the Supreme God declares will happen to you. You will be driven away from human society, and will live with wild animals. For seven years you will eat grass like an ox and sleep in the open air where the dew will fall on you. Then you will admit the Supreme God controls all human kingdoms, and He can give them to anyone He chooses. The angels ordered the stump left in the ground. This means you will become king again when you acknowledge that God rules all the world. So then, your Majesty, follow my advice. Stop sinning. Do what is right and be merciful to the poor. Then you will continue to be prosperous."

The Forester laid the Bible on his lap again, digesting this in his mind. His brow furrowed. "Was I so different," he asked aloud. "Was I so different at all? I didn't have the same riches and power, but did I show enough mercy to people in need? Was I fair in my judgment of others? Was I so blind?"

His throat tightened. He reached on the table to touch a sugar bowl that was made of brown clay with his daughter's hands. A slightly misshapen teddy bear perched on top and acted as a handle on the lid. She had beamed when she gave it to him, but he had nearly been too tired to even notice the gift of love it had been. He had forgotten it next to his recliner, but his wife took it and placed it on the center of the table.

He hadn't been untrue to his children or his wife. He always told himself he had to work hard to give them the things they needed, but the truth was that he was young and full of energy, and that the need for wealth, position and some kind of power seemed like the thing to strive for. A tear rolled from his eye as he lifted the tiny, brown, misshapen bear from its resting place on the sugar bowl base. "My family and God should have been my business. I was away too much and focused on my job even when they needed me."

Suddenly, he leaped from the chair, and with a cry that came from his core he raised his hands to the sky. "Lord, forgive me!" He fell to his knees and wept until he heard a baleful whining from the dog who had come crawling to him on his stomach, looking to him with soulful eyes. He reached out to the friend who had stood by him for these six years, never complaining, showing him true love without asking for much in return. He put his arms around the dog, pressing his face into its warm furry neck. Together, they lay upon the wooden floor, the dog's heartbeat thudding against The Forester's chest until he felt some peace return. When he finally rose and washed his face, he said. "It's a good day for a walk with my dog."

He opened the door to his cabin and stepped out on the modest porch, stopping a moment to take in the trees and the old narrow gravel road that sloped down into the valley fields before rising up again and curving left, back toward the forest. The road divided in the lowest part of the valley; bearing right led eventually to a village. The Forester had a unique view from his porch of much of the valley and the mountainsides rising around it. In this spring season the fields and mountains were an almost electric green. "God's paintbrush does some good work." The Forester took in a deep breath, feeling the cool morning air fill his lungs.

It was Sunday, the beginning of a new week, and somehow the beginning of a new feeling inside. He felt glad to be alive in body and soul, and celebrated by picking up a well-chewed stick that rested on the side of the cabin. He whistled, and his dog came running, pouncing around his friend, tail wagging in furious circles. The Forester smiled and threw the stick ahead of him, watching as the chase was on. Again and again the game repeated—the dog bringing the stick back, chomping on it mischievously, and keeping it out of the man's reach for just a moment before dropping it at his feet and bowing down on his front paws and begging for another round. They walked as they played together, making their way little by little down the road into the fields. Time effortlessly slipped away. Finally, The Forester said softly, "Enough." The dog bounded about, hoping The Forester could be encouraged, but he watched the stick disappear into the backpack and knew it was time to move on.

He raced into the field and began his second great game, Great Hunter of Wild Things. The Forester's face creased in honest joy as he watched the dog sniff with great focus until he gained a scent and shot away in a blur through the grass. The dog moved in zig-zags until he finally stopped short, burying his nose in the still short grass and digging with quick, intense thrusts of his front legs. He finally came back with a mole in his mouth, dropping it at the man's feet. "How do you do that?" The corner of his mouth lifted to one side in a wry smile. It was the same each time—the dog dropped a small animal from his mouth, always unharmed despite being wet and frightened, and The Forester would watch it scurry away into the grass, shrubs or leaves. His dog never chased his prey twice. The one conquest was proof enough to his friend that he could provide. Satisfied, the dog continued on the path, head held high and tail waving.

The two walked easily together as the early morning turned to late, and eventually they came upon a knoll that rose from the valley fields. When they reached the summit, they sat on a bench The Forester had built some years back. Just a few feet away was a pit lined with stone, and inside its bowl shape were ashes and pieces of blackened wood. It was an especially private place. Now and then, The Forester would cook some wild game for himself and the dog, but not often. He had never wanted to hunt and relished the idea even less now. Ironically, his one close friend usually brought game to share, the man from town being the hunter instead.

The Forester remembered his friend's words, "I'm taking you home." He came to visit twice a month, bringing supplies and a few hours of companionship. It was nearly the only human contact The Forester allowed himself—it was all he seemed to want, but he did look forward to it. His friend didn't understand this self-imposed exile, but he accepted it, and The Forester was grateful.

He pulled trail mix and a chunk of solid bread with cheese out of the pack and ate, tossing bits to the dog lying nearby, panting and mouth wide in a dog grin. He chewed slowly, tasting the hearty grain and the bite of the cheese. He closed his eyes to fully experience it then opened them again to drink in the mountains in the distance. Massive white clouds floated leisurely over them, the sky holding a pale blue sheen that sometimes turned bright against the electric green of spring and the shadows of the looming mountains. "How many people have tried to capture this on canvas or with a camera?" he asked the nearly laughing dog. "Some of them come close, but they just can't catch it like the artist who made it in the first place, eh?" The dog rested his head on his paws.

They came here every Sunday that weather allowed in the spring, summer, and fall. Each time they would sit—The Forester still and feeling all that was about him. Today, he let creation seep into him like water through mesh that filtered out everything cloudy and left him clear. His heart filled with love for the Creator of all that lay before and around him, a love he had not known since before his wife had passed.

He didn't think anything or anyone could ever match the love he held, and still did hold, for her in his heart, but what he felt now filled his very soul. There was the power, warmth, love, and safety as a child walks with his father, holding on to that strong secure hand. His senses were keener, his outlook on life richer. He somehow knew he was almost ready for something . . . almost ready . . . almost.

"Let's go home, boy."

Chapter Three

That afternoon he went to his shed and brought out a few gardening tools, placed them in a handmade cart, and headed for the piece of land he'd chosen for this year's vegetable bed. Each year he let the old plot rest and tilled a new area, spending time to turn sod over to reveal new and rich dark soil, picking out stones where he found them. He always placed the stones around or within his rock garden, slightly expanding that area and sprinkling some new seeds.

He pulled bits of grass that were trying to take hold and moved to toss the handfuls in the field a very small distance from the cabin. When he did, he hesitated, remembering a walk with his dog last fall. He had suddenly noticed the grass, and gathered seed heads of what obviously were many different kinds. "Well look at that!" he'd muttered. "I thought grass was just grass."

Thinking back to that time, he chuckled and tossed the handful back to its brothers. "Like us, or even like you," he announced to the dog lying nearby. We're all different, but we're all part of the same family somehow." His dog scratched behind his ear as though this was something he'd never considered before.

He was finished for the day, the sun now setting low. He carefully cleaned each tool and placed them all back in the shed.

That evening, he settled down in his favorite chair, picked up the Bible, and opened again to a random page.

All mankind are like grass . . . The Forester raised his eyebrows and kept reading, *and all their glory is like wild flowers. The grass withers and the flowers fall, but the word of the Lord remains forever.*

He closed the book and placed it gently on the end table. Some grasses withered while some flourished. Some seed heads were full while others remained scant. "Lord, why must some suffer so and others not?" There was only silence in the cabin and the rhythmic breathing of the dog. The Forester stared off, deep in thought, until heaviness pulled at his eyelids. He laid his head back for only a moment. . . .

He found himself sitting on the bench he had built by the old oak tree in the forest. He was looking up at a brilliant light of many colors, the colors swirling and forming a sphere. As bright as the light was, he didn't blink or shield his eyes; he felt a calm—a peace and joy. Thoughts filled the air in words but perhaps more like music that he could hear as words. The notes drifted to him and formed impressions. The musical words were powerful yet gentle. They came from inside him and yet everywhere around him.

There are those who say they love Me, but they are not pure of heart. They, I ask much of. But there are those that are innocent and pure of heart. They, I ask nothing of for I have received from them what I have asked. They have My blessing. What is suffering to others is borne by them with My grace.

The light and voice faded, and The Forester blinked his eyes. He must have fallen asleep so suddenly that he was unaware of it. "Now I understand," he whispered. Dreams like this were coming more and more frequently, but were they dreams? They didn't feel like dreams to him, although he had no other explanation. There was a reality to them and a purpose instead of random bits tossed together in any number of ways. His grandmother had said she had "visions" and had told him he had "the gift" as well. He shuddered remembering it. It sounded like something from a witch doctor or the kind of thing that people got locked away for.

The first time she had mentioned it to him was when he was seven. He spent many of his summer days at his grandparents' home, where his grandfather raised pigeons in a small outbuilding in the back; his grandmother kept a lush grape arbor that seemed an impossible oasis against the row upon row of small houses, all neatly packed one against the other with barely a front lawn at all, never mind creeping green vines full of plump fruit. That particular day found the young Forester sitting cross-legged in front of the radio, listening to the story of Jesus' crucifixion. He felt searing grief and ran crying uncontrollably to where his grandmother harvested fruit. She put the basket down, and he buried himself in her arms, sobbing, "Why did they kill Him? Didn't they know who He was?"

He felt her warm embrace as she tried to explain, but the reasons she gave didn't seem like reasons at all. He could no longer remember how she had tried to explain what had happened, but he did remember her lifting his tear-stained chin in her wrinkled hand. He remembered her smiling sadly until her hazel eyes, so much like his own, filled with tears too. "You have the gift and the burden, my boy. If you take it as gift or burden, well, that will depend on you."

He wasn't sure what she meant.

Now, nearly alone in the cabin, The Forester was amazed that he never thought of other events in his life as related to that moment at all. Now that he thought about it, or more accurately, *felt* about it, he knew there were certain times in his life that had the same flavor, like the time he went swimming when he was fourteen with a group of friends. He dove into the fast-moving brook although he was afraid and couldn't really swim, but he wanted to fit in so much. The water pulled and poured over a small dam next to an abandoned mill. He had broken the surface of the water, bulleting down and then moving back up, but he lost sense of where he was. He began to flail and finally came to the surface, splashing and gulping for air. Fear had left him weak, though, and he found himself dragged under again by the fingers of the current. When he went under for the third time, the pressure from his lungs and the panic left him, and peace and calm were there instead. Then he heard it—a chorus of voices singing. It was as beautiful as the musical words in his dream. He wanted to stay there, feeling the safety and hearing the sound of the voices, but the next thing he knew, he was gasping, water gushing from his mouth, his friends around him. "Are you okay?"

"I'm okay." He didn't tell his friends about the voices, and he'd claimed weeds caught his legs as he was swimming, that he'd thought they might be snakes, and he'd panicked. Later, he'd told his grandmother the truth.

She clapped her hands together. "You heard the angels!"

"Do you think everyone hears them if they die that way?"

"Love, I think anyone can hear them if they let it happen."

"Even if they're not dying?"

"Oh, I know I hear them sometimes, and I'm not dead yet."

"Anyone can hear them singing?"

"Not always singing, but certainly messages to guide, to tell you what you should do to experience a good life." She clenched her fist like she was squeezing an orange. "You need to listen to them to *really* feel life."

He knitted his brow. "So is it a gift or not? You said I had a gift. But if anyone can have it, it doesn't seem special at all."

She huffed gently. "Anyone can be given a gift. Not everyone receives it. And what will you do with it? Some take a gift and hide it in the closet or even throw it away. Some take a gift and do marvelous things with it."

"What am I supposed to do with it?"

His grandmother laughed and pulled him against her dress covered with tiny flower print. He smelled her warm, powdery scent that he knew he would never forget. "Don't worry about it, Boy. Just live and listen. Live and listen."

Then it occurred to him. "What have you done with yours?"

She looked at him with sparkling eyes. "I grow things."

The young Forester looked out the window at the lush grape arbors and the flowers in their shade. "You grow things? That's it?" He widened his eyes when he heard the words pour out loud, more rudely than he realized, but he relaxed when he saw her crinkled face crease even further in a knowing smile.

"That's it. That's a lot." She poked him playfully on the nose as she would have if he were years younger. "I don't only grow green things you know."

When the young Forester was growing up, he spent most of his free time with his grandmother. He supposed she did raise him more than his own mother did but still. . . . He slowly spoke his next thoughts, "It just doesn't seem like much of a gift. Why would God want you to grow things?"

"Why wouldn't He?" She pushed him gently back and started for the kitchen to make supper. "I don't ask why, Boy. I just do what I'm told. If you're smart, and I know that you are, you'll do the same. Things unfold as they should when you listen." She tapped her left ear. "Now go out there and tell your grandfather dinner will be ready in about half an hour."

The Forester looked around the cabin. It had gotten dark, and he plied the fire with some wood to take the chill out of the late spring night. He turned his chair a bit more towards the fire so he could watch the flickering flames. They danced, lulling his mind into emptiness again. There was no present. There were no surroundings. He sat motionless, eyes transfixed on leaping colors. . . .

He found himself on the side of a mountain, climbing up its craggy, steep cliffs. There was a great weight upon his shoulders and turning, he saw an enormous loaded pack. He was aware of a great hunger and thirst, and he raised his head to look above him at the summit. "Lord! I can't climb this mountain—it's too high. There is no way I can carry that pack when I'm so hungry and thirsty! Help me, for I truly love you with all my heart."

When he said this, he found himself standing on the summit overlooking a great plateau. Not far from him was a large wooden table, and standing in front of the table were four people. Two of them came forward. They lifted the burden from his back, and he felt as though he could rise into the air. Then they led him to the table. He looked to the right and left and saw his younger brothers. A woman approached him and gave him water to drink. There was sweetness with a trace of mint that seemed to linger afterwards. He looked at this woman and saw his younger sister. The four of them sat at the table. As soon as they had done so, a plate of exotic foods was set before him, and he ate until his hunger was satisfied. When he looked up, he saw the woman who had given him food was his youngest sister. They all sat together then. Although not a word was spoken, he felt their love for him and his love for them. Then he looked up into the bright sky that seemed to shower them with its light, and he felt the greatest love of all.

A loud pop from a burning log jarred The Forester awake. He caught his breath as he thought of the dream he'd just had. His brothers and sisters had all passed away years ago in a plane crash on their way to a family reunion. He had taken ill and had stayed home. He put his hand to his face. "I miss you." Still, he felt a clear comfort in the dream. But what was happening to him? He felt flooded and tired even though he had been napping all evening. It was time to surrender and go to bed.

His eyes popped open the next morning and took in the light without the disorientation of his typical morning fog. He felt the cool morning air welcome his skin as he slipped the covers back and placed his feet quickly and firmly on the wooden floor. His dog raised his head quizzically then sat up suddenly like a guard caught off duty by the Queen Mother. The Forester laughed and got ready for the day. He must have slept particularly well. He almost couldn't remember going to bed. He left the dog in the cabin and jumped into the Rover. He had some very specific things to do today.

He walked along the main trail, taking note of trees just in the distance with red marks on their thick bark. Each time he saw one, he stepped off the path to where they stood like silent sentinels, wrapped a tape measure around the trunks, and entered figures in his log. He checked what he could see of the leaves and branches for insect infestations as well. He was pleased to find mostly healthy trees.

His last task in the study area was to fill small plastic bags with soil samples. He had placed the last one in his pack and thrown it over his shoulders so he could head to another site when the sound of voices rose gradually through the forest. His hand gripped the pack strap and he stood still, catching one particular voice as it grew louder, heading in his direction. He thought to move back into the brush until they passed—it was what he usually did when hikers came by—but something in the voice washed over him and stirred a feeling in his chest. The woman's voice broke into a hearty laugh, and it seemed to be his wife's laugh. He remembered when something struck her funny she would laugh so loudly that people would turn and look at her, surprised and annoyed at first until the scowls melted into smiles of their own when they saw such joy on her face.

It pulled at him, this woman's voice. His feet started moving toward the sound although he tried with every fiber in his being to stop himself. His pace quickened, and his heart pounded within his chest. He saw them.

They were just seating themselves on the bench under the dead oak tree. "Mom, I'm thirty years old. I'm a grown man. Could you just call me Michael or Mike? Mike would be great. I like that."

The woman laughed again. "Mikey, don't be silly. There's no one here to hear me anyway, and besides, you'll always be Mikey to me. Can't you give your mother that?"

She handed him a sandwich and a thermos. He took both, smiling at her in a defeated way. They began to test the sandwiches silently, sitting there side by side and looking about them. The birds were in fine chorus and squirrels jumped from limb to limb in the canopy and chattered their displeasure.

The Forester watched from where he stood hidden. He watched her lift the sandwich and bring it to a beautiful mouth. As she chewed, her large brown eyes moved admiringly over everything around her. They were wide innocence set in a fair-skinned face. She had dark auburn hair streaked with just a touch of gray, and although there wasn't much gray there, he knew she must be in her fifties at least, unless she'd had her son when she was very young. That auburn hair fell just past her shoulders. She brushed a bit off the shoulder of her loose jacket and brushed crumbs from her jeans then settled back into eating, granting a smile and a flash of her large dark eyes to her son. He smiled back and tapped her on the shoulder, pointing ahead then to where a deer could be seen between the trees in the distance.

The Forester saw what caught their attention, but he couldn't look away from the brown-eyed woman. She reached in a bag by her side slowly and came out with a camera. He marveled at her stealth, but it wasn't enough. The deer there knew hunters well enough since hunting was invited and even encouraged on state land. A raised camera or gun didn't seem very different to the animal, who bulleted away with a breathy snort.

The Forester took that moment to gather his courage. He walked forward, swallowing the guilt as he thought of his wife. "Hello," his voice croaked.

The hikers jumped up and faced him. His forest ranger's uniform put them at ease. "It isn't hunting season, but they're smart enough to know something manmade when it's pointing at them and that it could mean the end if they're not careful."

The woman stuffed the camera back into her bag while her son reached out his hand and lit his face with a wide smile. "I'm Mike. This is my mother, Christa." She smiled too and took The Forester's hand. Her hand was warm, small, and soft. His own hand tingled from the shock of the contact with strangers. That's really all it was, he told himself.

"We're attempting a trek to the next town. Do you know how far we have to go from here?" She tilted her face a bit when she looked up at The Forester, and the lump in his throat refused to give way. He swallowed hard.

"Just stay on this path for another two hours or so and it will take you to within a few feet of the road that leads to town. From that point, it's probably half a mile to walk into the town on the road—you'll see the signs." He hesitated. "There are nice clean restaurants and cabins for rent at the base of the mountain if you want to eat and stay the night."

"That's exactly what we plan to do." She nodded to her son, who was looking again at the bench they'd just been using.

"Did you build that bench around the old dead tree?"

"Yes," The Forester smiled, "just recently."

"Great job! It was good to sit and eat on a bench with room for your things."

"Thank you." The Forester looked at his handiwork.

The woman took her son's arm, linking it with hers. "The grounds around it are quite lovely. You must have put a lot of thought and love into your work. I see you were careful to keep the trilliums safe."

He said nothing for a moment, but found himself drowning in the doe brown eyes. "Yes." He shook his head a bit to break the trance. "It has special meaning for me."

She turned to her son. "Mikey," and then seeing his eyes roll she rolled her own, "*Michael*, could you pick up the rest of our things and pack them up?" He nodded and walked back to the bench.

"Do you live in state?" The Forester asked.

"Yes. About thirty miles from here. In Albany.

"I lived just sixteen miles away from there some years back!"

"If you're ever in the area, stop in and say hello."

"I certainly will. Does your husband ever join you and your son on these trips?" he blurted, and when he saw the pain cloud her eyes, he wished he hadn't spoken.

"My husband passed away a few years ago, and this is my first venture into the forest—and a wonderful one, thanks to my son." She turned and looked at him putting the last small items in the pack. As he did, the clouds that had covered the warmth in her eyes lifted. Her lips pulled back in a slow, admiring smile that was so deep The Forester felt he was basking in front of a warm fire.

"Okay, Mom. All set."

"Thank you, Michael." She turned back to The Forester and held out her hand again. "Well, we're off. It was nice to meet you." Michael came up and shook his hand as well, and The Forester stood silently, watching that lovely creature of God walk out of his life, possibly never to return to it. His heart tightened, and he pulled a well-worn wallet out of his back pocket. He stared at it then slowly opened it to reveal a picture. It was a woman in her early fifties. The woman in the picture smiled up at him. His rough fingers passed over the smooth surface, tracing the hair and cheek of her face. He let out a soft sigh, closed the wallet, and tucked it back in place.

He adjusted the pack on his shoulders and headed for the next research site. He found himself doing more than he needed to do, checking and rechecking spots, and humming out loud. When thoughts invaded his mind, he hummed louder. Eventually the sun threw longer shadows from the surrounding trees, and he knew it was time to go.

In his quest to focus, he hadn't noticed how far up the path he'd gone, and he had a long trek back to the Rover. He was weary, not from the work, but from his encounter with the hikers and the feelings he thought had died in him long ago.

He put his fingers to his temples and made little circles, trying to find the control he had worked so hard to build up in his life. He hadn't allowed himself to cry much even after his wife's death; instead, he had become bitter and sought solace in alcohol and his small apartment until he had crashed. Humanity had seemed cruel until his friend had introduced him to new hope. He had grasped it eagerly, but still hadn't let go of the fear of pain. Fear of people. Fear of opening his heart again.

The thoughts, the dreams, the emotions he was experiencing were growing rapidly, like a train on a track with no brakes, gathering speed. He was afraid, but stillness in his deepest heart told him he couldn't do anything about it.

Suddenly he noticed he was back at the Rover, and try as he might, he couldn't remember walking the entire length back.

Chapter Four

The Forester discovered he was a young soldier again in the Army. He was in Europe and working on cleanup detail. Suddenly, a voice he didn't recognize yelled, *"Put on your helmet!"* It was a hot day, and since the shells they were picking up from this firing range were dummy rounds, they hadn't seen the need for the steel helmets. The Forester felt the resistance inside of him when he heard the order, but in his dream, he saw his hands move and felt the helmet being set in its rightful place. He didn't want to disobey any orders today and get in any more trouble than he'd already been in.

Another soldier nearby cried out and flung a grenade far from him. "It's live!" The man's voice was as strained and pulled as his face. The Forester could see it in remarkable detail—the terror in the eyes and the grenade sailing through the air until it struck an iron rail, exploding. Men were thrown to the ground, some seriously injured. The Forester felt the helmet torn from his head then he too was thrown to the ground. When he rose, he could hear men calling, "Medic!" Others screamed in pain. He ran to help load the injured into the trucks that would transport them to the hospital.

One of the medics grabbed his arm. "You'd better get in there too. How much pain are you in?"

The Forester felt confused. "I'm fine."

"Well, you're bleeding from your back, Private. You must have been hit with some shrapnel. I'll have someone look at it."

They took off his jacket and shirt, finding a minor wound. They cleaned it and sent him on with the other injured for a closer look back at the base.

Early the next day, the men on detail during the explosion were sent to a room designated for investigations. When it came time for The Forester to give his story, he explained where he was standing and that he put on his helmet when he was issued the warning just before the live grenade was thrown. The two investigating officers sat neatly behind desks, looking at each other with raised eyebrows, and then one turned back towards The Forester. "Are you sure that's where you were standing?"

The Forester described once again exactly where he had been.

"You couldn't have been standing there—it was near the center of the explosion. Everyone nearby was seriously wounded and no one but you has reported any warning. No one gave a warning. You must be confused. Have the medics keep an eye on you."

He was dismissed and went back to his room to change into his fatigues and join the rest of the squad. A corporal sauntered in carrying his steel helmet. "Boy, you were lucky. Your helmet is completely destroyed. If you hadn't had it on, you wouldn't be here. Before you head out, go down and put in for a new one."

The Forester looked at the torn steel. Who had yelled the warning? He knew he'd heard the voice. The words had been plain.

The dream shifted; he was still in the Army, but later in time. He felt himself pulled from one place to the other, until the fibers of his being seemed to reassemble in a chair facing the chaplain. He was having trouble with some of the NCOs exploiting the new recruits. Favorites were given passes for a night out, but others saw no relief for months. Some new recruits had tried to fight back and were found severely beaten or were shipped to a different company.

The young Forester had gone to the chaplain and told him what was going on. The chaplain had listened, leaning forward, grim faced then had immediately called the Commanding Officer and explained what he had heard was happening under his watch. The Forester couldn't hear the words in the dream, but he watched the expressions on the chaplain's face change in minute detail. His eyes widened when the Commanding Officer slammed the phone down.

The chaplain pushed his chair back and fixed his eyes on The Forester's. "I see what you're dealing with." He picked up the phone and dialed again. "Captain, this is Colonel Murphy. I have a direct line to the commanding general of this battalion. Should I use it?" He covered the mouthpiece with one hand and smiled at The Forester. "I think you'll find a change for the better in your company from now on."

The Forester felt himself moved forward in time again to the next day. He was granted a three-day pass—his first in three months. That night as the young Forester left his room to begin his leave a soldier he didn't recognize grabbed him and threw him against the wall with such force that everyone in the adjoining rooms ran out to see what had happened. The strange soldier held the young Forester against the wall, one of his hands clenched at his throat, the other ready to smash into his face. Suddenly, The Forester felt a peaceful strength. He looked into the soldier's eyes and spoke in a voice that didn't seem his own: *Why do you do this thing? I do not know you.* The soldier's hands dropped instantly and clutched his stomach as if in great pain. The Forester shook his head with disbelief as the man ran from him, bent over and now holding his mouth as if he would be ill.

The young Forester straightened himself from where he'd been forced against the wall and saw everyone's eyes on him. Not one person looked any less than amazed, and The Forester understood why. What had he said? They weren't his words but they came from his mouth, and why had they had such an effect on a man hell-bent on beating him or worse?

The Forester woke from his dream eyes searching the dark with the same questions then that he'd had at twenty-one years old. He had nearly forgotten those events, and the dreams brought them back with new clarity. He didn't want to think of them. He rolled over and heard the breathing of his dog beside the bed. He focused on the rhythm of it, hoping it would lull him back to sleep, but the images and questions kept invading where he tried to find peace. After two hours of struggling, he groaned and rubbed his palms into his eyes. The dog lifted his head and looked at him curiously, also heavy with sleep. "Oh, why am I flooded with this," he grumbled to the dog. "If it doesn't stop pouring dreams, I'm going to have to build myself an ark!"

Chapter Five

The weeks rolled by. For the first stretch of time he could remember, he didn't want to go into the forest. Each time he did, he kept imagining the woman with the doe-like eyes, her laugh washing through his memory like a warm shower. He tried focusing on his duties, tried getting lost in them as always, but that only worked for a while. Eventually his thoughts brought him back to her face, the way her hands moved when she spoke. "I don't even know this woman," he said to the trees. "I'll probably never see her again."

He did a better job avoiding thoughts of his dreams—perhaps because there was little room for that with the doe-eyed woman taking up so much room in his brain. He saw her in the purple trillium flowers that were starting to go by. He saw her when he looked at something he had built or posted in the forest. He especially saw her when he glimpsed a deer in the field at the edge of the forest—just like a woman who was far away in his mind's eye—disappearing with a flash into the dark forest just as he noticed she was there.

His friend came to visit on schedule, bringing supplies The Forester had requested. He set the bags down and slapped his reclusive friend soundly on the back and they embraced. "I brought some special coffee this time. It's dark and strong. I figured good for a mountain man!" He drew himself up and brought his arms down like a body builder, flexing his muscles, as The Forester laughed.

"I'm sure that's just what I look like. How about having a cup then?"

"If you promise to visit me soon." The Forester's body tensed, and his friend looked away quickly. "Well, at least promise to think about it."

The Forester breathed in slowly and deeply, closing his eyes and willing each muscle to loosen. "I promise to think about it."

The two men settled on the cabin porch with hot coffee in hand, gazing out over the fields and forest. The Forester had a question he struggled not to ask, sipping his mug of the coffee that really was good enough to savor in his mouth a moment before swallowing it down. Suddenly, he set his mug on the side table. "I actually met some people not too long ago. . . ."

His friend nodded and sipped from his own mug, eyes closed with reverence.

"A widow and her son. Auburn hair. Maybe in her mid-fifties. Son's name was Michael and they're from Albany."

"Really?" His friend's mouth twitched at one corner, and he opened his eyes, looking calmly ahead.

"Know anyone like that?"

"Well, you're not giving me much information to go by."

The two dropped into comfortable silence and looked ahead of them at the greens and browns of nature all around. Birds sang loudly, sometimes flying close enough that they could hear the wing beats. The dog slept on the porch next to them, his feet moving in some kind of dream. They sipped the coffee until there was no more, and The Forester looked into the bottom of his cup thoughtfully. "Think you could find out who she is? Christa. Her name was Christa."

His friend met his gaze with barely concealed sparkling eyes. "I'll see what I can do."

When his visitor drove away, waving and with a quick beep that set the dog barking furiously, as it did every time the man left, The Forester returned to the porch. It was a warm, beautiful, clear night. The sun had set behind the distant mountain, and he rocked back and forth in the old rocker, feeling better than he had in weeks. He'd think about visiting.

He gave the dog his supper and thought about eating too, but when he stopped to feel, there was no hunger there. He wandered back to the porch to watch the stars come out, seemingly one by one until they suddenly covered the entire heavens. "Beautiful." He tried finding the two dippers and then the different constellations, but he chuckled at himself for trying again. His knowledge of the night sky was limited, and he didn't understand why he kept trying even though he hadn't learned anything new about it.

As he gazed up, a brilliant sphere seemed to shoot down from the sky and hover perhaps one hundred yards away from him. Although it was shining brightly with dazzling shades of blue, it didn't bother his eyes at all. He stared into it, unable to move, and in a flash it shot forward, engulfing him. He found himself high above the Earth, and as he looked down his heart broke and great sorrow pressed inside him. Below him was chaos and suffering, people screaming in anguish and looking up, pleading for relief from their pain and imprisonment from this place. There were men, women, and children of all ages, all races. He felt their pain as if it was his own, then with no warning he was back in the chair.

The sphere was nowhere to be seen, and the dog looked out curiously to where it had first been. "Did you see it?" The Forester whispered, and was glad no one else was there to hear him. It was as if God had let him see and hear what He could see and hear for just a moment. It threatened the peace and beauty The Forester had back in his grasp for too short a time, and he set his mouth tightly and felt his fists clench.

It wasn't the first time the sphere had engulfed him. It had happened once before when he was twenty-eight. It changed him for a while. He spent more time with his wife and their first daughter. He tried to worry about money less. . . .

His wife noticed the change and seemed happier than she had ever been. Remembering the smile on her face warmed his heart. She seemed so rarely without a smile then. How did he end up, then, back in the rut where he started?

His grandmother was frail by the time he was almost thirty. She no longer picked grapes or went out to visit much, but The Forester had visited her to share his experience.

"You're being reminded." Her old voice cracked, and she shook a finger towards him. "You need to make some changes."

"How do you know this isn't my mind playing tricks on me?" he grouched. "Maybe you and I are just . . ."

"Crazy?" She finished his sentence with her eyes, blue-veiled with age, wide in defiance. "I may be many things, Boy, and some might say I've had my crazy days, but I know what I know and I see what I see! Do you see what you see, or will you turn your eyes away?"

That night, The Forester had shyly told his wife about the sphere. To his surprise, she didn't think he was crazy either. She took his hand and her eyes shone with tears of joy. "That's what made the change. I don't know what it means, but it's wonderful."

Her smiles had faded as his resolve to keep his focus faded too.

It was the week of July fourth, and The Forester had two weeks free. Normally, he would have stayed at the cabin, working on his vegetable or flower gardens, taking walks, and playing with his dog in the quiet, playing solitaire or reading. This year, though, his friend made a special visit to remind him of his promise.

"You said you'd think about visiting."

"I promised to think about it. I thought about it, and I don't feel ready."

"Look, I haven't pushed you, but it's been almost seven years; you can't grieve her forever. You have to move on."

The Forester shot his friend a pained look. "You know it's more than that."

His friend nodded. "I know, but you can't keep running from what's inside you either, or what you've done, or what you haven't done, or what you're afraid to do." He took The Forester by the shoulders and looked directly in his eyes. "Come visit. I'm not saying to leave this behind now and forever. I'm just saying to come visit. One step at a time."

Just days later, his friend picked him up and he was on his way. The ride to his friend's house took about forty-five minutes, and as more and more houses started to appear along the road, The Forester noticed how many new ones had cropped up since his last trip through the area. They dropped his dog off at a small kennel along the way, the dog looking woefully at The Forester as he walked away and promised to return soon.

His friend chatted while he drove, stopping the car to let a line of people cross the road toward a baseball field. "T-ball," he explained.

The Forester looked at one little girl running from her mother's hand and to the bench where some of her friends must have already been waiting. She reminded him so much of his youngest daughter when she was small—the jaunty stride and the bouncing curls.

"Did you know I never made one of my daughters' school concerts or plays? Not one."

His friend reached over and patted his shoulder roughly. "We can't change the past."

They left the town road and sped down the highway, finally reaching his friend's large Victorian house, which seemed in very good repair. His friend was capable of everything from plumbing to painting.

People of all ages were setting up tables in the yard, and some of the young boys were chasing the girls around, the young ladies letting out screams laced with giggles. The Forester's friend parked the car out of the way on the far right of the grass, waved to his wife, and moved briskly to the trunk to unload The Forester's luggage—one small bag. "Come on in. We'll put your things away, and I'll introduce you to anyone you don't know yet."

The Forester looked at the number of people milling about; his head swam and his stomach knotted. Suddenly it all felt unreal, like a dream.

Could he be dreaming again? Sometimes it seemed so hard to tell. The children running and laughing seemed to move in slow motion. He saw one of his friend's neighbors raise a tablecloth and snap it, but it hovered, lingering there in the humid July air, settling slowly on the tabletop. There was a pressure in the Forester's head like something significant would happen. He felt excitement and dread at once. *Maybe I shouldn't have come. I'm crazy. I don't belong with these people.*

His friend showed him to his room. The Forester followed mutely and automatically, placing his things where they would be most convenient, washing his hands and face, combing his hair— seemingly completely average to anyone looking at him despite the fear inside.

Everyone greeted him, and the warmth of it gradually melted the ice in his veins. A few small children came up to him shyly at first, then with boldness, pulling on his roughened hands and asking him questions. It wasn't long before he had a circle of children around him, asking him to re-tie a shoe, wanting to know if trees really got sick, asking if he'd ever been chased by a bear, and did he want to play jump-rope? He handled the questions deftly and began weaving fictional stories about trolls living in the forest and little princesses who would befriend them, to the children's squeals of delight.

His friend's wife walked over, parting the sea of little ones like a feminine Moses and sent them on their way with a playful shooing motion. "It's almost time to eat. Just amazing how children are drawn to you!"

"I never really thought I liked children even though I love my daughters," he said with a wry smile.

"Well, as I recall children have always loved you. No matter where you go they stick to you like metal filings on a magnet!" As if on cue, a little boy ran up with hopeful eyes. His friend's wife laughed and shooed him again. "Go tell the guys on the grill what you want to eat, and let *this* man have his supper too!"

She had just finished speaking when a car pulled tentatively up to the house, stopped for a moment, then pulled onto the side lawn where other people had parked too. The Forester felt a bit of ice return to his veins as if there was something important about the car. A woman stepped out and looked quizzically around, a wide smile spreading over her face as she decided she was where she belonged. The Forester's heart leaped. It was the woman from the trail. "I believe you two have met," his friend's wife cooed, "but why don't I walk you over there and reintroduce you?" The Forester felt a stare, and he turned to see his friend placing burgers and hot dogs on waiting plates, winking to his friend as he did.

Somehow he moved forward to greet her. His heart filled. She was more beautiful than he remembered. His friend's wife reached out to grasp the brown-eyed woman's hand. "Ms. Thomas! I'm so glad you could come."

"Please call me Christa," she said, her eyes searching The Forester's face. "Well! It's a small world. You're the Forester we met not long ago! It's so good to see you again." She hesitated a moment and knitted her brow. "We told you our names, but I don't think you told us yours now that I think about it."

The Forester looked into her brown eyes that seemed like melted chocolate, and he never wanted to look away. "Michael," he said. His voice croaked a bit, and he cleared his throat.

Her voice was soft. "Oh. Like my son," then she grinned a devilish grin. "Well, it isn't like I'll be able to forget you then."

The forester looked to his side to say something to his friend's wife, but saw she had vanished. He turned back to Christa with what felt like a moth beating madly in his chest. "Did you enjoy the rest of your hike?"

"It was wonderful, and so were the days spent in town. You were right—the restaurant and cabin were perfect and the people who own it are very kind."

A shout rang through the warm summer air, and they both looked quickly to see the forester's friend waving them over. "If you want to eat, I'm serving!"

"Well then, Michael. Shall we?" He walked with her toward the grills and the tables, marveling at how strange and amazing his name suddenly seemed. He was Michael. He was Michael . . . and she was Christa. He liked the sound of it.

They settled with their food. The little boy who had approached the forester so hopefully before had found his way to the same table, looked about him, and pointed like a tiny king making a decree, "The very young, the young, the older, and the over the hill." His mother gasped when her son's pointer finger landed squarely on the forester, but he waved away her concern with a chuckle and turned to look into the child's bright eyes. "I'm so sorry you can't be over the hill. It's beautiful there." The boy scrunched his face with disbelief, and the forester leaned forward, careful not to push his shirt into the juicy burger and special potato salad his friend made from a recipe handed down for three generations. "How would you like to hear about it? I'm not supposed to tell young people, but I suppose I could tell you if you promise not to say anything about it when you leave here." The boy's eyes widened with wonder, and he only nodded, so the forester began:

"Once there was an old man who said to a group of young boys, 'Hey, throw me the ball and I'll pitch a few to you.' They stopped their game of catch and looked at him, laughing. Then one said, 'you're over the hill!' They all turned away and continued playing as if the old man was invisible.

"As you can imagine, the old man felt really hurt at this, so he walked away, following a narrow path he'd never noticed before that led up the side of a large hill not too far from the small village. After walking for hours, the old man crested the hill and, looking down on the other side, saw a beautiful sight. The trees were small and bore fruit of many kinds, and the grass was a beautiful and a rich deep green. The air was full of dragons of many colors— gold and jade, pink, blue, and some having all the colors of the rainbow. The dragons played among the small trees biting off some of the fruit, happily eating. Others soared into the sky higher and higher, doing all sorts of acrobatic stunts, snorting fire, and chasing each other about.

"The old man was marveling at this fantastic vision when one of the smaller dragons of gold with blue wings landed before him and began to speak. The old man shook with fear. Then, hearing the musical tone of the dragon's voice and hearing words, he relaxed and was no longer afraid of the creature. It said to him (or actually it sounded more like music than a voice as we know it), 'Would you like to sit on my back and have me show you the wonders of the world?'

"The old man's heart leaped with joy and excitement; he had never told anyone that this was his greatest wish and fantasy since he was a small child. He climbed upon the dragon's back and grabbed on to a knob-like scale that came out of the back of its neck. He held on for dear life as the dragon beat its blue wings and rose into the air. He soon found himself high above the clouds; the water and land seemed to rush by below him. When they came upon a place the old man really wanted to see, the dragon would fly lower, and the old man could look upon the wonders of God and man.

"He saw great forests and oceans, animals, and fish of all kinds. He saw buildings of all sizes, some magnificent and some plain and cozy. He saw people of many colors—white, yellow, black, red and tan. Soon they were back where they had started. When he set his feet back on the earth, he heard the dragon say to him, 'you may stay until it is time for your last journey. With us, you will want for nothing. You need only say and it will be done.'

"Then the old man spoke to the dragon, 'Oh beautiful dragon, why didn't I know about you when I was a child and I wished for this with all my heart?'

"The dragon replied, 'You were not then old enough to be over the hill.'"

With the flight of fancy concluded, the forester lifted his burger and took a large bite, chewing slowly and relishing it as he pretended not to notice the little boy's wide open mouth. The people seated around broke into applause, and he felt a knot return to his stomach. He hadn't felt self-conscious at all when he was telling the story and everyone listened, but now he felt all eyes on him and heard the deafening thunder of their hands coming together. It was meant well, he knew, but he couldn't raise his head. Then he felt a soft hand take his and give it a gentle squeeze, and he looked into Christa's admiring (he thought) doe eyes. Then he felt able to look at the friendly faces around him, smiling and approving of . . . of what? A silly tale?

"Where did you hear that story? I don't know it." Christa finally said.

"I just made it up."

"When?"

"Now."

She breathed in deeply. "You have an amazing imagination."

"I don't know where they come from really."

"Maybe you should write?"

"Oh, I've been a business man and worked in the woods. I don't have the stuff for that."

Christa drew her body up, filled with resolution. "Stories are my business, and I know talent when I see it. You certainly do have 'the stuff.' If you don't want to do anything with it, that's fine, but don't fritter away your life because of false modesty."

The forester's eyes flew open wide. "False modesty?"

"Oh, come on. On some level you must know you have talent." She winked to soften her observations. "I'm saying it this way because I feel . . . comfortable with you."

"Don't argue with a woman!" the forester's friend piped in from further down the table. Now it was Christa's moment to turn a bit red. "I distribute books for publishers," she explained, but the forester could only hear, "I feel comfortable with you."

Chapter Six

The days flew by. He and his friend had taken long rides on old back roads and hiked through some of the local woods. The forester had felt a huge sense of relief being with the trees again, away from groups, and he still felt uncomfortable around people he didn't know. One day he did agree to go to a restaurant with his friend and his friend's wife. To his surprise, they had once again invited Christa Thomas. He loved her face, the way she laughed, but he felt the wrenching memory of his wife pushing forward at times. He began to look for signs of her in Christa's face and manners and found plenty. When he did this, he could relax.

When he was alone with his friend later that evening, he said, "I really like this woman, but I feel that somehow I'm being disloyal."

His friend put his hand on his shoulder. "She's gone. You have to *go* on. She'd want it."

"But there's so much I should have given her, so much time I wasted. . . ." The forester broke freely into tears in the companionship of a friend who he knew would understand. He wanted his small cabin, his dog, his forest.

It wasn't long before he was back in the car with his friend, heading home to his solitude. After stopping at the kennel to pick up his whirling dog, his friend dropped them both off. The car slipped out of sight. The dog still wore his leash and collar, and the forester bent to remove them. "That must feel good, like taking off a suit and tie," he said. The dog looked up gratefully before dashing off and giving the surroundings a thorough check.

The porch was waiting like a dream. He set his suitcase down and sat in the old rocker, looking out at the distant forest and hills. He still had one week of vacation left. Well, there was enough work around the place to keep him busy.

Truly, there was plenty of work to do, and the days passed by. He slept soundly and dreamless each night, and by the time the first day of work in the forest arrived, he was in a good frame of mind.

A week later, the dreams began again.

The forester had a physically grueling day clearing large limbs after a severe thunderstorm with winds like he hadn't seen in years. He nearly collapsed in his favorite chair and fell asleep almost instantly.

He found himself talking to two ministers. He was trying to expand his business, hoping to create jobs. The ministers had heard about him and what he was trying to do and asked for a meeting. They picked him up from the office and drove with him to an area restaurant, asking questions along the way. Similar to the dream with the Army chaplain, the forester could see the two ministers' faces in sudden and intense detail, nodding their heads with approval.

They arrived at the restaurant, and before they left the car, one said, "We should pray for the success of your venture." As they bowed their heads and started the prayer, the forester collapsed in the back seat. His whole body felt as if it was expanding. Energy surged through him as if he were a wire conducting pulsing electricity, but the power of it was more than his body could stand. He gasped for breath and was unable to speak above a whisper. The two ministers didn't know what was happening until they opened their eyes and stopped praying. They rushed out of the car and opened the back door, helping him out with great care. By then he was fine, though. To his surprise, it was as if nothing had ever happened the moment the prayer stopped.

When he explained as best he could, the two ministers became very excited. "You're destined for something special," one said, gripping his hand tightly and pumping it as if they had just met. They wanted to know more, but the forester had nothing more to tell. He thought of his grandmother and the things that had happened since he was seven years old, but he pushed the memories away. There was nothing more to tell these men. He was nothing special and certainly not in the category of these God-fearing men. When they persisted, he asked them to change the subject, and they ate their meal together speaking only of business. He had really had a vision, then—a vision that should have helped people who were struggling. Why had it gone wrong?

The forester awoke, a frown on his face. He hoped the dream had stopped and that he was truly awake. "These are like a biography of my life," he whispered. "How much more will there be? Why?"

It had taken all of two weeks to get the main path and the rest areas back to normal. One day he worked in the area of the old oak tree. He put extra effort into seeing it was clean and that the new season's flowers growing nearby were free of strangling weeds. It was high noon when he sat under the oak on the very bench he'd built. He was hot and sweaty from working, and he laid his head back on the trunk, feeling a cool breeze caress his brow and wash over his body. He sighed. His friend would be coming to visit soon even though it hadn't even been quite a month since he had dropped the forester off after his visit to "the land of people."

When his friend came, he talked a great deal about Christa Thomas. "She had us over for dinner, you know. She's quite a business woman, that one!"

"She owns the distribution company, she said?"

"Well, she did own it before her husband died. It was something they did together, but her son, Michael, has taken it over. Apparently she's stayed on as the treasurer and to do the marketing and PR because she *likes people*. Imagine that, pal? She might be able to teach you a few things.

The forester grunted. "Maybe I could teach her a few things too." He waved his hands to show the beauty around him.

"Maybe you could at that."

"Who's to say she would want to teach me anything anyway?" His heart seized as he waited for his friend's answer. There couldn't be any question that his friend knew he was fishing, but they both played along without drawing any attention to the process.

"Oh, I'd say she's keen on seeing you again."

The forester waited impatiently for more words that his friend willfully withheld. They rocked and the dog, as if mirroring the forester's feelings, approached his friend and whined plaintively.

"She put on a beautiful dinner," he said at last. "She made something called beef roulade mit spaetzli and some very nicely flavored red cabbage. German heritage," he explained, as if the forester had asked.

"Did she mention me at all?"

"She may have a few times—like when she wanted to know about your past, and how she wanted to know how long you'd been working in the forest, and if you had a history of telling those 'marvelous' stories, and why you are still single when you're obviously so handsome." His friend rolled his eyes as the forester smiled shyly. "Yes, I'd say she's keen to see you again."

Chapter Seven

The forester found himself whistling more than ever as he worked through the days, walking with what seemed like ceaseless energy. He welcomed the crisp air and pulled it into his lungs like a welcome friend, releasing it and feeling the way it fed his body. He could nearly feel the oxygen coursing through his veins.

Today he was working on a newer, less-used trail. He grinned at the challenge of a limb that was dangling precariously across the path. It was dead wood that the tree had shed by choice or by force, but on its travel to the ground, it was caught in the arms of smaller trees trying to grow below it. Hikers walking here could duck under it, but the forester would rather it be on the ground, beginning to rot back into the soil and offering shelter to so many small, usually invisible creatures that scurried and crawled. He'd have to pull hard to dislodge it, so he took a firm grip, and set his teeth against the strain, using his own weight as a tool.

He tugged, feeling the smaller trees sway with the effort, not wanting to easily give up their catch. The wood on this dead branch had some beautiful twists and turns to it. Suddenly he imagined Christa

Thomas watching him as he worked. "That's such beautiful wood, Michael! Do you think you could make me a . . ."

His feet slipped out from beneath him on the wet leaves just as the trees let go of the dead limb they had been keeping. He felt a pain, and then a bright light that flashed in his head.

He found himself on different ground—hard like concrete or pavement. Young boys were laughing and holding him down, trying to take off his clothes to hang them in a nearby tree. He was struggling with every ounce of strength he had, but he couldn't throw them off and keep his pants up too. He finally threw back his head and screamed, "God! Help me!"

"Let him go."

The forester couldn't see who said the words, but he heard the voice with shock. The voice was calm and strong. The boys laughed louder as they succeeded in pulling his pants down almost to the knees. The voice came again with no change in tone. *"You shall let him go."*

The boys stopped and looked, allowing the forester to also look for the first time. A young man stood nearby, tall and dark, but without a hint of menace. He looked much like a Greek boy who had lived not far from the school grounds where the attack was happening, but the Greek boy had died at least a year ago, and this person seemed older, stronger.

The boys rose to face the dark man. "We were just fooling around!" The forester watched them walk away, and filled with relief, pulled his pants back up and rolled over to reach for his shirt. He raised his eyes, intending to thank the dark stranger, but he was nowhere to be seen.

The scene blurred, and colors mixed together in swirls, with the familiar tugging sensation the forester had in some of his dreams. Again, he and the colors re-collected in a different scene. He was in a doctor's office. He was disoriented. He heard voices in his head along with the sweet music he had heard when he was drowning. He heard the doctor's voice speaking to someone, his wife.

"I can't explain it. It's as if he has just lost the will to live and his body is shutting down. It's a severe depression."

His wife's voice came back, soft and fearful. "But what is he depressed about? Nothing has happened . . . things are the same as they've been. . . ."

"Sometimes these things are just chemical."

"I've been with him for all these years and he has *never* been depressed."

"In any case, I'm afraid he'll die if we don't get on top of this. I'm prescribing something for him for the next six months. I'll need to see him frequently at first to make sure he's doing all right on it."

The forester couldn't hear them anymore because of the voices in his own head. "God is coming, God is coming," the voices said. He thought God was coming for him, but in just months, his wife was diagnosed with her terminal illness. It was not he that was to die, but her.

He felt pain in his head again and put his hand up to it, feeling a large bump but no wet blood. His eyes blinked open, squinting at the light filtering through branches, and realized he was back in the woods lying on a cold wet bed of leaves. Pushing himself up slowly, he eyed the dead limb that had gotten the better of him. He sat there in the cold, just breathing. His grandmother had said it was a gift, but was it? Was it a gift to know you would lose the one you loved more than your own life? Was it a gift that she had to struggle to buoy him for months before struggling with her own illness? He rubbed his face. His hand was cold, but it felt good when he brought it to where the limb had struck. He didn't know if he could take knowing again—losing again.

He should just remain alone and not know. He rose on wobbly legs, picked up his pack, and slowly walked back down the path until it joined the main trail. He followed it awhile longer and came to the oak tree and the bench. He sat down there, and after resting, felt well enough to walk the rest of the way to the Rover.

After dinner, he sat in his chair and took up a pencil and pad of paper, jotting down his dreams and visions over the last six months. As he did, he noticed many of the strange or important events in his life happened every seventh year. He was born January first at seven in the morning. He found Jesus at seven years old. He almost drowned and heard the musical voices at fourteen. He married his wife when he was twenty-one, and he was saved by the mysterious voice and attacked by the soldier the same year. He first saw the bright globe at twenty-eight. His first daughter and second daughter were born seven years apart. He started a new business at forty-two and tried to start a program to help the unemployed at forty-nine. He heard the voices, music, and suffered the depression along with his wife's diagnosis at fifty-six. "What will be next?"

The dog ambled over and looked at him seriously. He leaned forward to whisper to his dog,

"The contract I signed for this job was for seven years. It's almost over. I don't want to face the world again."

He thought of the vision that Daniel had explained to the king. At the end of seven years the king would return to his kingdom. Would he be given the same chance to have what he had lost? Did he want it? He rose abruptly, shook his head, and said, "This is crazy."

He clucked to his dog and opened the door. It was late September and the leaves were bright. The days and especially the nights were cooler, and the winds of winter would howl through the leafless trees soon enough while the fields would wear a white blanket of snow. He would have to leave it just before Christmas. His wife had died on the twenty-eighth day of December. Again, the number seven.

He climbed into bed that night trying to shake the strangeness that seemed to stay around him like a mist since he'd written the dreams and visions down on the paper. A movement caught his eye, and he turned to see a white-footed mouse sniffing about the bottom of a small bookshelf. He watched it poke about quickly and expertly until the twitching nose found a trace of bread that the forester hadn't even noticed was there. It was a bit of bread crust from a snack his dog had taken toward his bed to savor in private. "Messy eater," the forester muttered of his pal, and the mouse stopped like a deer in the headlights. "Oh, you have nothing to worry about.

Remember, the meek shall inherit the Earth!" The mouse sat back on its haunches, nibbling the bread and keeping a wary eye on the man regardless of his promise of no harm.

The forester pulled the covers up to his chin after turning off the light, and looked out at the nearly full moon. "Please. No more dreams."

It was not to be.

He was on a cobblestone road walking toward a large building. In front of this building were seven steps that led to seven doors. He walked up these steps and approached the first door. As he stood before it, a scene appeared. He saw a young child newly born. He tried to walk in, but could not. He then moved to the second door and saw a young boy crying and kneeling with his hands over his face. The third door showed a boy swimming in a stream that flowed up into the heavens. The fourth door showed a man looking down on a scene of suffering and turmoil. The fifth door showed the same man with hands stretching out to heaven and a beam of light, like a rainbow, showered down upon him. The sixth door showed an older man looking up and listening to a voice. The seventh showed the Earth again in great turmoil. The oceans boiled, and there were great fires and suffering of all kinds. But, within all of this, appeared a bright dot of light. The door vanished, and there seemed a moment of peace, but then an eighth door appeared, but it did not open right away. A powerful light seemed to filter out behind the rim then the door melted away, revealing the Earth once more. A great battle was taking place. In its midst was the little dot of light. Suddenly, from the heavens above appeared a great white sphere of light and behind it, many smaller ones. They fell to the Earth below, and there was a brilliant flash. When it was gone, there was only darkness, and where the Earth once hung in the heavens, there was nothing but a small light that seemed to grow in size and brilliance as he watched.

It all faded away. He found himself on his knees before the great wall. A voice spoke, "It is not yet time, but soon."

He woke with a start. He wished more than anything that he had his grandmother to talk to.

Chapter Eight

"You always seem to know when I need you," he said to the dog. The dog wagged his tail, and his ears moved and twitched as if he was listening intensely to his friend's words. The brown eyes were wide and pools of wordless emotion. The forester bent over and hugged him. "I love you too." Then, widening his own eyes, added, "How about a walk?"

The dog leaped from the porch, ran around in a circle, stopped short, and barked for his friend to hurry. The forester burst out in a hearty laugh. What joy could come from such a simple thing? They struck out together for their sanctuary on the hill. The days were flying by now. Before, one day had been like another, deliciously safe and warm and in solitude. Before, he didn't have a care, and he didn't think of the day he would have to leave. Now it was looming just ahead of him. Here it was, already the last day of November. Each day now tugged at his heart, and the old fears grew. He felt better outside, but whenever he returned to the cabin, he'd pace the floor, wanting to scream out, "I don't want to leave! I'm happy here."

He stopped walking for a moment and stared ahead, reaching into his pants to pull out his wallet once again, to flip the leather fold open and look at the face in the picture. "I've lost so much, but the most precious thing of all was you. You were the light in my eyes, the very breath of my life. Now that I've finally found peace again, why do I have to lose it?" He lifted the picture to his lips and gently kissed it. That face of the past smiled up at him forever, with so much warmth and kindness and openness in her eyes. As he'd done so many times before, he ran his finger across the smooth surface of the photo, touching the chestnut hair and the smiling cheeks. He grudgingly put the photo back, refolded the wallet, and returned it to his back pocket.

His friend had invited him to their Thanksgiving dinner, but when the forester declined despite a fine and spirited debate, his friend settled for bringing him some turkey with all the dressings and a pumpkin pie the next day. "Christa Thomas made this for you." He had said, searching his friend's face. The forester had refused to meet his eyes.

"Tell her thanks."

He had eaten the dinner after his friend had left that evening, and he was grateful. When it came time for a piece of pie, he looked at it a long time, finally and slowly taking a bite. He could taste the nutmeg. He liked it when there was a good strong flavor of nutmeg. He closed his eyes and thought of a conversation he'd had with his friend once. "God asks us to choose life if we can. I would really love to see you choose it."

When the forester returned from his walk, he brought out the last piece of pie and savored every bite. He had chosen life, but a sheltered one. Now he had to trust and step forward in that trust.

The winter snows were piling up on the week of Christmas. The forester's daughters called this kind of smooth, untouched white snow "vanilla milkshake." He chuckled, thinking of them as little girls clutching their plastic sleds and plummeting down the hill crying out between breathless giggles, "Daddy! Watch!" He'd go down with them sometimes. Other times he had to be the "boot seeker" when, invariably, at least one girl lost a boot in the deep snow.

There wasn't much for him to do now. The hiking trails were closed for the season. Occasionally he would put on snowshoes and check on some of the trees or study the signs of different animal tracks in the snow—large romping rabbit tracks and tiny squirrel feet sometimes mingled with the even smaller mice trails with tell-tale thin lines drawn from the long tails. Afterwards, he would return to the cabin that was blissfully warm from the fire. He made his last trip out to the forest just days ago. A new man, not long out of college, would be taking over his post, his cabin, in May.

The forester's friend visited the cabin for the last time and invited him to stay with them until he found a place of his own. Since the forester hadn't spent money on much other than food for the last seven years, he had built up an impressive nest egg. His friend had helped him invest some of it in good stocks, which meant he'd be quite comfortable in retirement.

"You've done well for yourself!" His friend spread his arms wide as if showing a bounty. "Think of it—you came to this cabin seven years ago without a penny to your name." He cleared his throat. "Of course, you didn't *do much of anything for seven years either.*"

The forester just smiled. "I did exactly what I needed to do."

"Well, you had what you needed, but I'll tell you, we're going to be glad to have you back in society."

"Oh, Dad! It's good to see you again!" His youngest daughter wrapped him in a hug and squeezed so hard, he couldn't breathe in. He only had a moment to recover when his oldest was taking her turn.

"You're such . . . *women*." He stood back and looked at them both in their Christmas finery. "When did that happen?" Of course he'd seen them since they were grown, but in his mind, deep in the woods, he still imagined them with bouncing curls and skinned knees.

Neither had children, but both worked with them. The oldest, Taryn, had been drawn to working at a children's hospital. He didn't know how she could do it; many of the young patients were facing probable death, but she found purpose and deep satisfaction in it. Sonya, his youngest, worked at a preschool. So it wasn't surprising to find the girls had conspired to bring a basket of children's books to the Christmas Eve dinner at his friend's house.

His friend's wife took the basket and kissed both on the cheek. "Thank you very much, girls!"

Sonya caught up one of the grandchildren in a quick surprise hug. "Our pleasure, Anne! It's the least we could do for having you and Don invite us."

She released the little captive, who fled with a smile to her grandmother. "Can I open my presents now?"

"Not yet. First everyone needs to visit and settle in. Then we have dinner. Then, good girls and boys . . ."

"And good men and women!" Don piped in.

"Yes . . . and good men and women, will get to open their gifts. Michael! Why don't you read a story to the kids? You tell such a good tale."

Taryn reached in the basket and pulled out a book. It was old. The Forester's eyes scanned the familiar cover, *Five Fairy Tales*. "You used to read to me from this one, Dad. Read them "Beauty and the Beast" like you used to read it to me."

The forester settled on the couch, with the two grandchildren nestled close. He read out loud to them, growling like the beast and making them jump. He closed the book at the end of the story and set it back in the basket.

"Could you tell us another story?"

The forester leaned back. "Well, I can, but this is a story that is very old and you can't find it in any book."

"Tell us!" The little girl's eyes were fixed on the forester's face.

It's about two little rabbits that looked an awful lot like the two of you — except much more furry. But one, named Fumbly, had blue eyes like you, Sarah, and Mumbly had brown fur like your hair, Jim. . . ."

While guests arrived and presents were added under the tree, and Anne, Taryn, and Sonja set the food on the table, he weaved his tale of a loving mother rabbit who taught her fumbling and mumbling little ones that they could succeed despite the physical issues they faced. He had just finished when Anne called out, "Dinner, everyone!" The forester looked up to see Christa Thomas standing in the room, smiling down at him.

"Another beautiful tale."

He couldn't do anything but beam back at her.

She reached out her hand. "Come on! Didn't you hear Anne? It's time to eat."

"Where is your son? I thought you'd be with him for Christmas Eve."

"He's spending this Christmas Eve with his fiancée's family."

They sauntered toward the dining room together to the sound of laughter and three conversations going on at once. "That doesn't bother you?"

She pursed her lips. "No. We'll have tomorrow morning, and anyway, I raised him knowing that he'd grow up and have a life of his own. Things change."

"You sound so matter-of-fact about that."

"What else can I do?" Her eyes sparkled up at him. "Sometimes changes are wonderful and sometimes they're hard, but if I'm to be alive, change will happen and I need to embrace it. I choose to live."

The forester stopped suddenly, making her stop too and look at him with a quirked eyebrow. "Did I say something wrong?"

He smiled at her. "No. No, you said something very right."

They said grace and ate. It had been years since the forester had sat with so many people and felt so comfortable. He didn't think of anything but the present moment and the love of the people surrounding him; he took in the sounds of many familiar voices, and the addition of one newly familiar one—Christa Thomas.

Her voice sang, clear and strong, as they sat around the tree after dinner, sharing some Christmas carols before opening the gifts. His voice harmonized with hers in his deep bass.

"Dad! I forgot how well you sing!" Taryn gasped after the first song was over.

Sonya winked. "He can cut a rug too, remember? Mom said they called him "Twinkle Toes" in the Army."

Christa looked at the forester with her mouth open. "How did a man as creative as you—the storytelling, the singing, the dancing—how did you end up in business?"

"I worked in the same business my father was in, and I never thought much about it," he shrugged.

"And then forestry?"

"That's a long story, but trust me, it's closer to creative than I can explain in words."

"I know we don't have time now, but maybe someday you can take the time to try putting it into words." She nodded to the children, who were starting to fret that they would never get to their gifts. "It took Santa Claus all year to make these presents and put them under the tree early for everyone here, so I'm sure it's okay that we waited that much longer to open them." She winked at them, and Don and Anne handed out the first of many gifts.

Anyone can be given a gift, but not everyone receives it. The forester heard his grandmother's words as if they had been spoken softly in his ear, and he looked ahead to see his grandmother leaning toward him, smiling warmly and with potholders on both her hands. She was holding a casserole dish with something steaming inside. It was like a still of her — a holographic image—her eyes fixed on his. He could look deep within her gaze and see the wrinkles and creases the large smile made around her eyes. She looked younger than when she had finally passed away, but still aged. Then a loud laugh broke his concentration. The image snapped away, and he blinked quickly to readjust. It had felt so real, and the warmth of his grandmother stayed with him like a blanket. He shot a look at Christa and the others around him, but they hadn't seemed to notice his lapse.

He watched everyone's faces as they laughed, sometimes the expressions melting from smiles into tears of joy at something particularly personal. Before long, Don brought out a large box filled with small packages and no names. "You were the one who started this idea years ago, Michael."

Christa looked questioningly in the box, and Michael gave her a guilty smile. "I don't think I'm the only one to blame."

"Everyone picks something from the box, and I'm going to warn you—the things are all ridiculous." Anne looked like she was chastising the forester, but a twinkle in her eyes gave her merriment away. "You pick what you pick, and then you have to do something foolish with what you get."

"It's like you put on a show!" one of the grand-children shouted.

"And, yes, Michael you *are* the only one to blame. He tries to say it was his daughters' idea years ago, but they say something different."

Anne unwrapped a fat rubber nose and Don pulled out a fake cigar. They looked at each other considering what to do then they tried to kiss. The big nose and cigar made this impossible, and the children shrieked with laughter as they pretended to try over and over. Don and Anne's son picked out huge red candy lips. He put them on then rose, asking who wanted a "big, fat, sloppy smooch," heading toward his children and chasing them around the room. It was so familiar that the forester looked at his daughters and tears filled his eyes. They both hurried toward him and surrounded him with their arms. "I'll never forget," he whispered.

"Neither will we, Dad," Sonya said. Taryn offered a tighter squeeze of agreement.

When they pulled away, he looked at all eyes upon him and the gift giving stopped. He mumbled gruffly, "Sorry. Tears of joy. Just tears of joy."

"Michael, there's no reason to apologize. In fact, now that you've drawn attention to yourself, I think you should be the next one up!" Don slapped his leg and waved his hand to signal that the box should be ushered toward his friend. The forester dabbed his eyes quickly and laughed, reaching in and unwrapping gigantic slip-on ears. He placed them carefully over his own, made a ridiculous face, and did his best to gambol around the room like Dopey in "Snow White and the Seven Dwarfs." When he got back around to Christa, he gave his best stupid grin, picked up her hand, and placed a loud kiss upon it to hysteria in the room.

Chapter Nine

"Michael! Breakfast!" Anne's voice cut into the forester's deep sleep, his eyes opening before his brain knew what was taking place. For a moment, he thought he was a child in his grandmother's house. A woman's voice was calling to him, and the smell of bacon and coffee drifted to his nose when he was nowhere near a stove to cook it. Then for a moment he thought he was at his beautiful little cabin, but his dog couldn't cook, and there was no cold nose to prod him out of bed. Then he remembered the night, and laughing, and Christa talking with his friends and family as if she'd always been there. In a way, she was so much like his wife it seemed strange that, as he was waking, he didn't think it might have been her calling. Somehow he never forgot she was gone.

He made his way down the Victorian staircase, feeling the wood and the form of the carved newels and banister as he went. It was good cherry wood. Probably very old and carved before everything was done with sophisticated machines.

"Merry Christmas! Someone slept well." Don helped his wife get the plates and handed one to the forester. There were eggs over easy, wheat toast, and bacon and sausage just finished cooking. A plate of stuffed French toast sat on one side of a Christmas centerpiece and a pitcher of maple syrup graced the other. "She doesn't have a date for New Year's Eve, you know."

The forester had been hungrily eyeing the bounty and trying to decide if he could possibly eat a bit of everything. He decided to be modest and only took one meat while everything else made its way to his plate. After a moment of silence, he looked squarely at his friend.

"As if you haven't already made plans for us?"

Don chuckled and Anne pushed some butter towards the two. "Don't worry, Michael, we have a *suggestion*, that's all. You have to ask her if you *want* to. We wouldn't just go and plan something like that."

He rolled his eyes but softened it with a creased smile. "So what would you call last night?"

"A good idea. Oh, seriously, Michael," she nearly pleaded, "that was different. It was a group of people getting together, not a date."

A date. How would he know how to date? After all those years with one woman, and they had been young when they met. It wasn't as if he'd had a lot of dates before his wife. It seemed almost ridiculous to date in your sixties. He thought of Christa's brown eyes and soft hands, the way those eyes sparkled when she laughed, and how she quirked her eyebrow when she asked him certain questions. Strangely, he had been starving, but now he didn't seem to want to eat much. He wasn't sick, but just didn't need to eat all of a sudden.

Anne's brow furrowed in worry. "Something wrong with the food, Michael?"

"No, Anne. It's perfect. I think my eyes were bigger than my stomach this morning. We did have that huge dinner last night. I'm not used to having so much at once." When he returned the untouched bacon to the pan, he suddenly thought of the dog. When he'd make breakfast, he'd share his eggs and bacon with his dog. He glanced at the floor where a food bowl might have been.

"Don, do you think you could recommend a good realtor? I think I should start looking for my own place."

Anne looked up with a forkful of egg and toast nearly to her mouth. "You know you're welcome to stay here as long as you need to. There's no hurry."

"Oh, I know. I don't feel rushed, I just . . . I miss my dog." When they both started to protest he said, "I completely understand about the allergies, and I can't tell you both how grateful I am for everything.

There aren't words . . . plus . . . " he spread his arms to take in the full table and stove, "I'd get too spoiled here. You know how she used to take care of me. She did everything but lay my clothes out each morning. When she was gone, it was a shock to take care of myself again. I think it would be pretty easy to slip back with you around, Anne!"

Don nodded sagely. "And you miss your dog and he can't be here."

The forester sighed.

His dog was staying with the family where he had been whelped. It wasn't that he wouldn't be well cared for or have plenty of company, but the forester missed the shaggy head in his lap, and the soulful eyes looking into his as he'd scratch him behind the ears. Just thinking about it made him almost feel the soft fur between his fingers. He had never thought to ask Christa if she liked dogs. He could ask her New Year's Eve. He chuckled inwardly. It seemed he'd made up his mind. "Tell me more about what you might 'suggest' for New Year's."

New Year's Eve found him in his room putting on his best suit, marveling at the shine on his new shoes, then standing in front of the mirror, staring at a stranger. He had worn little other than work boots for seven years, T-shirts and flannels with tough jeans or his khaki work uniform. He vaguely remembered looking this way once, but it was so long ago, and he was different then. He hoped it wasn't vain, but he thought he looked better now in many ways than when he was younger. When he was a businessman, his belly had rounded out and was easily noticeable under a suit jacket. Now the fabric fell the way it would on a man years younger. He was fit from his work in the woods, broader in the arms and narrower in the waist. His salt and pepper hair was still mostly black, with the white hairs mainly around his temples. His grandfather had kept his mostly black hair well into his seventies. "Good genes, I guess," he whispered to his reflection. Some of his curls were wayward, so he grabbed a comb and some of his friend's hair groom and worked them carefully into submission.

When he came downstairs, Anne threw a look at Don and clucked approvingly. "You clean up really well, Michael! I think our little Christa is going to be a goner."

When they approached Christa's door, her son met them with a small brunette by his side. He looked into the forester's eyes as he shook his hand, but the forester found nothing but warmth and happiness there. "This is my fiancée, Bridgette." The small woman shook his hand too and looked just as pleased.

"We're going to spend the evening with some friends," the younger Michael smiled a bit wider, "but we thought we'd see you kids off first!" Laughter filled the room, and the forester looked up in mid-laugh to see Christa descending the staircase. He was barely aware of the younger Michael offering them all drinks, and he couldn't answer. Her auburn hair was swept up in the back and shone like copper, revealing her still lovely white neck and shoulders. She carried a sequined black bag in her hand and wore a small tiara on her head.

Finally, the forester found his voice, but it was husky with emotion. "I know this is a cliché, but you look like a princess!"

"I thought I'd better look like one if I'm on the arm of a prince," she winked.

"We are, after all, going to the fanciest place we could find." Don added. "Hob-knobbing with royalty, so why not look the part."

They had a nearly two-hour drive, the forester sitting with Christa in the back of Don and Anne's compact car. The intoxicating scent of her perfume seemed to weave its way into his brain. It was subtle but undeniable—a bit spicy or woodsy with a hint of spring wildflowers. He thought of the spot by the great old oak tree where he'd first met her and breathed in deeply, the smell bringing him back there in a wonderfully intense flash.

When he let out his breath in a deep sigh, Christa reached over and squeezed his hand. Feeling her question, he tilted his head toward her and whispered, "I was just thinking of the first day I saw you. The perfume you're wearing reminds me of that place."

"That's good," she smiled and looked away. "That is a beautiful place to remind you of. I suppose you're going to miss it?"

"I already do. It was hard to leave the peace."

"Didn't you miss all of this?" She pointed out the window at the passing houses and lights.

"I don't know why, but no. I had my dog, and all the animals I'd see while I was working in the forest, and it's safe to say God is with me all the time. I didn't have the chance to get really lonely."

"Oh." Christa's eyes appraised him deeply, but he couldn't see what conclusion she reached, if any.

"But he's going to be looking for a place around here, Christa," Anne added quickly.

"Oh?" Christa said again. He thought he saw something light up in her eyes. Was she glad he was staying? She shifted in her seat to face him as much as she could in the arms of the seatbelt. "What kind of place are you looking for?"

"Not anything large, and something a little out of the way. Somewhere my dog will be happy."

The four of them began discussing dream homes and retirement homes, and the difference between what people might want for a home and what they really needed. He was pleased to discover she was ready to downsize too, and that, while she had specific wishes like a kitchen that was set up for fine cooking and a place large enough to serve friends and family dinner, she also seemed happy with the idea of a simpler way of life.

Don slipped in a CD of 1940's Glen Miller classics, and the *Moonlight Serenade* began to play its romantic dance strains. For the first time in eight years, the forester wanted to hold a woman in his arms. Not any woman, but *this* woman. *She's so beautiful, so graceful,* he thought. *Maybe I'm falling in love with her?*

They finally pulled up to the club, Don dropping them off at the front of the building while he found a parking spot nearby. It was a mansion-like building, a splendid old place with pillars in the front, framing the large double doors. The doors were beautifully carved, and as he always had to do, the forester reached to let his hands explore the nooks and crannies of the wood. He loved wood, alive, and in art. True art like this seemed like an honor to the tree that gave its life for it. "This is original I'm sure," he told Anne and Christa as Don finally approached, his breath puffing a bit in the chill last night of December.

The men extended their crooked arms to the women, who primly accepted their escorts and allowed themselves to be lead into the splendor.

They stepped into a large hall with a deep rich wine-colored carpet, and the walls were mostly neutral but with splashes of the same color. Beautiful paintings of stately men and women hung there, unsmiling in their importance, but work beautifully done. The forester would have rather seen paintings of animals, but he could appreciate them.

"I wonder why it was a crime to smile back then," Christa mused aloud. The forester burst into a laugh. It was as though she'd read his mind! A man in a tuxedo greeted them and asked for the reservation names, checked his list, and said the table was ready, but there was time to tour the building if they wished. "Everything is decorated authentic to the period of the building."

They moved together from one room to another, marveling at the beauty and design, but the forester was mostly enjoying the feel of the soft arm linked with his and the way he could feel the air move when she moved, lifting that perfume to his senses again. "Michael! I'm so glad you invited me here. This is . . . it's . . . it's *enchanting*."

They had reached the doorway of the dancehall, still empty but ready to greet them soon. A stage was set ready with chairs and musical instruments, and from the center of the ceiling hung a large mirrored ball that reflected white lights, landing everywhere like stars. Moved, the forester swept onto the floor and reached out his hand to Christa, who laughed with delight and joined him. He hummed bars of music while he danced her around the empty room, finally leading her back to where Don and Anne waited, bemused.

"Shall we go to the dining room now, ladies?" Don took Anne's hand in his and raised it to his lips. "You aren't the only romantic in the room, Ol' Boy," he quipped.

"I learned from you, friend!" The forester patted Don on the back, and they all moved back to the dining hall and the tables of white linen, topped with polished silver and crystal glasses. The room was about half full, with more people streaming in after the Forester's party. A tall man rose from a nearby table and practically ran to Christa. "Hi there! I haven't seen you at church lately!"

The forester gaped a bit at the man's sudden outburst, but Christa seemed unperturbed. "Carlton! I didn't know you'd be here." She gave the tall, gangly man a gentle embrace then turned to the others to present him. "This is Carlton Freeman. He's a member of my church and a good friend. Carlton, this is my date, Michael, and our friends Don and Anne."

Carlton approached the forester and slapped him a bit hard on the arm. "You have a beautiful lady there! You're a lucky man!"

"Yes, I am." The forester smiled at Christa with a sudden realization that Carlton had spoken as if he were speaking to a couple, and he felt a deep sense of pride. It was then he noticed a part of the man's skull on the left side was caved in.

"I would have given you a run for your money if I wasn't married already, Joe!" Carlton's voice belted out through the noisy crowd. "If I did that, though, my wife might take a frying pan to the other side of my head!"

Christa laughed. "Oh, Carlton! You're hopeless. Your wife is beautiful and sweet."

"Yeah! I know! I keep getting myself in trouble with my big mouth, though!" He grinned pleasantly through his entire speech, like smiling was the most natural and only thing he could do. "Well, I'd better get back to the gang! Nice to meet all of you!" He reached out his hand and roughly shook Don and Anne's hand, then reached for the forester's.

When their hands met in the grip, a feeling of great sorrow and physical pain rushed through the forester, nearly knocking him over like a wave of cold ocean water. He gasped and stepped back slightly, feeling the pain within this brusque, tall fellow.

"Handshake too hard, then!" Carlton nearly barked apologetically. "I can try it again!"

"No, no." The forester didn't think he could stand feeling it again, knowing what was hidden inside this man. "It's a great, strong handshake you have there, Carlton. Nothing wrong with it."

The forester's brow furrowed.

"I'm sorry if that hurt," Christa apologized after Carlton was seated again at his own table. Carlton was in a car accident some years ago, and the head injury left him a bit like a little boy. He's still good and kind, but he doesn't always know how to control his words or his strength."

"Is he . . . pain . . . does he still feel any pain from it?"

Christa widened her eyes. "If you picked up on that despite all the smiling, you're really intuitive. He feels pain all the time, and a ringing in his left ear that never seems to go away. He hates it and says it's a horrible high-pitched whine, but unless you're one of his closest friends, he doesn't tell anyone about any of that." *So that could be where the pain in him comes from,* the forester thought, *but what about the sadness?* He didn't know if the sadness was Carlton's feeling or his own.

For a moment, he wanted to tell her about all of it—the dreams, the visions, his grandmother, unexplained knowledge of things—just certain things—out of the blue. For the first time in eight years he not only wanted to hold a woman, but he wanted with a suddenly intense longing to *tell* her what he feared telling most. But this was their first date, and a happy occasion.

He took her hand. "I'm glad Carlton has people like you who understand, and who knew him before and can remember him then and accept him now."

They settled at their table and he let the urge slide away, forcing his senses back into the wonderful flavors, smells, and sounds all around him.

Later, they moved across the dance floor in beautiful synchronicity, the steps coming back to him as if they had never left. Holding her was so familiar, so much like holding his wife. The band played a few of the older big band dance tunes, and when one ended with the forester very gently dipping his lovely date, the previously crooning singer said, "And now something a little more modern!" The band began a song with a wild beat the forester had never heard, and he started walking from the floor.

Christa grabbed his hand, eyes shining. "Oh, Michael! Let's stay."

"I don't know how to dance to these."

"It's not hard. You just do whatever the beat tells your body to do. There's no way you can be wrong!" She laughed out loud and started to dance in front of him, moving her feet and her arms, moving her head so the gentle curls along her face bobbed. He closed his eyes for a moment and felt the music then let his feet start to move. He felt stiff and ridiculous at first, but his daughters had been right when they spoke about his being "Twinkle Toes" in the Army. He couldn't resist music once he let it take hold. After two songs he was feeling more comfortable, and Christa's beautiful face, flushed from the exercise, was all he needed for encouragement. *I'm glad I'm in better shape than I was years ago*, he thought. *This takes a lot of stamina!*

In time, the singer made a different announcement. "Fifteen minutes to midnight, folks! Save your drinks for a toast."

Ten minutes. Five minutes. One minute, then ten, nine, eight, seven, six, five, four, three, two, one....HAPPY NEW YEAR! The band played *Auld Lang Syne* and people were toasting and kissing each other. "To a happy and prosperous new year." Don raised his glass and they each did likewise.

The forester turned to face Christa, and she smiled coyly. "Happy New Year, Twinkle Toes." He kissed her gently and turned to see Don and Anne looking like proud parents.

When the night was over and he saw her to her door, he felt like a schoolboy.

"Michael, I had a wonderful night."

"I will never forget it," he responded. *Should I kiss her?* He didn't have more than a moment to wonder because she stepped forward and tipped her head towards him. He met her halfway, their lips touched, and he swore he could still hear the bells calling in the New Year.

Chapter Ten

Don and the forester were looking at pages of homes for sale online. He'd had limited knowledge of computers before his wife died, but the eight years since found him completely separated from technology. He was amazed, watching Don find things so easily. The screens changed in a snap, and he was able to see the outside of homes and inside, and even in some cases tour them as if he was walking through. Things had changed so much!

Many places were too large, and some needed more repair than he wanted to take on at this time in his life. "I don't mind adding some nice details with my woodworking, or even landscaping, but I don't want to completely renovate," he told Don.

"I don't mean to keep steering you to the fixer-uppers," Don grimaced. "I just can't *help* but see the potential, you know? And the prices on them are so good, you just can't beat them."

The forester knew his friend had a longstanding addiction to "potential." This wasn't the house they had lived in when the forester took his job taking care of the trails, and they'd owned three before this. They were all sad relics that he and Anne worked hard to miraculously breathe life back into. Anne gamely pounded nails and tore out old sheetrock and painted and stained alongside her husband, but even the forester could see how hard it was for her to live in homes that were always in progress and then, just as they were at the pinnacle of beauty, be taken away to a wreak again because Don couldn't resist the next project.

The forester looked hard at his long-time pal. "I hope this isn't making your mouth water for another one, Don. I don't think Anne could take it."

His friend grinned wryly. "Oh, I'd love to do it, but don't you worry. I know she's had enough. I was hoping to live vicariously through you."

After looking for at least two hours, the forester found a few that had potential. One was even a cabin; although it had a bit less land than he'd hoped for, there was state land surrounding it, and no one would build next to it—at least not as long as he lived. He pushed his chair back and raised his arms in a long-awaited stretch. "Well, I've narrowed it down. I guess I can call tomorrow and make an appointment to see them." He studied his fingernails a moment. "You know, do you think it would be too forward to invite Christa to look at them with me? I don't want her to think I'm rushing her into anything, but I'm feeling ready, Don . . . I'm feeling ready. It seems silly for me to buy a place she wouldn't want to live in someday—you know—if things go well. But I do need to find a place so I can have my dog again and so you and Anne can get back to your normal routine."

"You're rambling, Michael! You already know what you want to do. So far your instincts have worked just fine, so if it feels good, do it." He looked off to the side as if considering, then added, "Although maybe you could at least ask her out for one more date before you do mention anything."

Later that afternoon, the forester stood with his heart pounding in his chest, listening to ring after ring until Christa picked up the phone.

"Michael!"

He breathed out in relief when he heard the joy in her voice. "I know we just saw each other yesterday, but I wanted to see if you'd like to have breakfast out with me Saturday. The weather is supposed to be beautiful, and maybe we could do a little sight-seeing together afterwards."

He nearly danced on the ceiling when she said yes.

"Well, I had been thinking about you too, and I have a question of my own. Would you like to come with me to church Sunday morning?"

He hesitated. He hadn't been to a church in some time—not since Sonya joined one before she'd moved from the area and had her baptism ceremony there. In fact, that had been the first time he and his wife had been in a church since their wedding day. He thought of the praying ministers from years ago and his strange reaction to them, and his heart seized. His daughter's baptism went smoothly, but. . . .

"It's okay if you'd rather not," Christa said in response to the silence.

"Oh no, I'd like to very much. It's just that it's been such a long time."

"Wonderful! If you don't mind meeting me at my house, we can walk to the church if the weather's going to be as good as they're saying."

"I haven't gone walking nearly enough since I've lived here," he said. "Getting out like that sounds perfect. And breakfast—if I pick you up at nine Saturday, would that be too early?"

"No, nine is fine. You do realize Saturday is the day after tomorrow?" There was a lilt of merriment in her voice.

"Well, yes! No! I guess I hadn't thought about how close it is. Is that too soon?" He slapped his hand to his forehead and was glad she couldn't see.

"No, Michael. It's not too soon. It would be lovely to see you the day after tomorrow."

When he hung up the phone, his mind raced. He would call the realtor tomorrow and see if he could make an appointment to see houses . . . when? He decided to wait until Monday to call. By then, he would have asked Christa if she even wanted to go, and if so, when she could join him. It was strange, stopping to consider someone else's needs and schedule. Later, he took a walk into town, stopped for a coffee, and chatted with the owner of the café. It was three miles to town from Don and Anne's, but that was nothing compared to what he had managed when he worked the trails. He imagined what it would be like Sunday, walking along, breathing in the fresh air, with Christa beside him.

When Saturday came, he drove Don's car to her house and found her casual but elegant and ready to go. "You like to be on time, don't you?" he asked, grinning appreciatively, and she offered him a hug.

"It's part of being in the book distribution business so long, I guess. Getting things where they need to be on time makes the difference."

"Yes," the forester mused. He didn't know many women close to his age who were business people like he had been, and it felt strange to walk to the car with someone who he wanted to hold in all her womanly softness, but who *felt* sharp and confident at the same time. He opened the car door for her, and she climbed in. "Don said you've stepped back from your company now? That you're helping with the accounting but having your son take over?"

She held her answer until he was seated and belted in the driver's seat beside her. "It's time. I've felt the need for a change in the last year or so. I know God has something else planned for me, but I'm not certain what it is. I just know that if I don't step out and free myself to do it, I won't be able to change when I need to."

"You don't seem nervous about this at all. I wish I had your faith."

"Don't you?" She pursed her lips. "It seems to me that it took a lot of faith to completely change your way of life from business to being a forester, and to embrace that for seven years even though I'm sure a lot of people didn't understand."

"I'd like to say it was faith, but it just happened, and I had no choice. Everything had been stripped from me. I had no options, and that was the only door that would open. That's how my entire life has seemed to be. I haven't had the faith I should have, really, but things just happen."

"Hmmmm." They rode in silence for a few moments as he felt her thinking about this. They pulled into the café parking lot and talked about their hunger, and she made recommendations based on what she'd eaten there before. He thought the topic of faith was closed until they had placed their orders, and she touched on it again. "So do you see any options now, or are you waiting until something just happens?" He blushed and she quickly added, "I know you've retired, but is there another life goal you see ahead? Something you'd like to do with your time?"

"I hadn't thought past finding a place to live. I don't know what else I would do now. It's funny— when I looked for jobs after I lost my business, people seemed to think I was too old to hire even then. What would people think of me now? I think business is out of the question. God closed that door in my face as hard as it could be slammed."

Christa smothered a laugh, trying not to spit her coffee. "It does seem that if you don't make the change you need to on your own, God kicks you forcefully out of that nice warm nest."

He never considered this before. Every change had been forced upon him and he'd struggled against each one. He even hated leaving the warmth of his nest in the cabin and the forest. The only reason he left was because the contract ended. He remembered pacing the floor there, nearly grinding his teeth with frustration that his safety was to be taken from him. He told her so.

"Well, maybe it's time to change that pattern," she slapped the table gently with one hand. "Follow where you're being led instead of resisting it." The waiter brought steaming plates—eggs Benedict for Christa, and a thick slab of ham, eggs over easy, and home fries with onions for the forester. "When did you get into business, Michael?"

"I started helping my father when I was a teenager. Then I went into the Army and married, and when I came back, I was drawn to forestry, although it was a fairly new field then, and there weren't many jobs. I went through quite a bit of training and worked part time for my father to pay the bills. When there wasn't any job open remotely close to what I'd been training for, I felt I had to be responsible and just fell into working for my father full time again. It was all I knew."

"What did you do before your teens? What did you love?"

He chuckled. "You already have a theory, don't you?"

"I do. Just testing it," she grinned.

"Nothing in particular. I loved to dance. I read comic books and I spent a lot of time in my own head, imagining stories. I was a dreamer, solitary. I took care of my younger sisters and brothers because home was a little . . . *crazy*."

"I see."

He waited for more from her, but it didn't come. "Well?"

"Well what?"

"Aren't you going to tell me if your theory was right?"

"I did notice you are very good with children, and that you understand what they want, and even need, to hear. You're a wonderful storyteller. I would say my theory was right on. Ever think about writing books for children?"

Now it was his turn to laugh so he had to try not to spit his coffee. "I think I told you I'm no writer. I don't even know how to type."

"Ah, but you're a storyteller. I think you could do it. You could learn the other parts. I could help you. Before you fell into business, you were a creative soul. Haven't you always felt it pulling at you?"

He stopped to think about it. He'd kept himself too distracted by the pursuit of money, things, social standing, but when he was in the forest alone he had felt compelled to take the dead branches and turn them into something beautiful, although he could also appreciate the beauty they made left to nature's way.

Then he remembered telling his daughters stories too—silly things that would come straight from his mind. He didn't spend a lot of time with his children, but when he did, those were moments he actually felt good about. They were moments that he felt their happiness, and the business world melted away. Since there were seven years between the girls, he had weaved different yarns at different times for each one, and they were the moments that he connected with them. They were the moments that he never realized he was recalling when he looked into their eyes now as grown women.

How is this possible? How does she do this? He thought. *I feel like she's no stranger, like I've known her for such a long time.* He had never been one to open up about his thoughts like this except to his grandmother and somewhat to his wife. He couldn't have loved either of those women more, but he still hadn't ever spoken so much of what was going on inside him. Somehow, over the seven years in the forest, he had been changing so gradually he didn't even realize how much.

"Michael, I know we're spending the day together as it is, but I was wondering if you would have dinner at my house tonight. I had no particular plans tonight anyway, and when you drop me off, you're welcome to just stay through until dinner is ready. You could watch a movie while I cook. That way you don't have to drive all the way to Don and Anne's just to turn around and come back just a little bit later." This time she blushed, and he nearly choked on a piece of ham hurrying to answer.

"I'd love to. Speaking of homes, I'm calling the realtor Monday to set up an appointment to look at several I like. I would really enjoy having you along. A woman's opinion on things never hurts."

The waiter came to ask if they needed anything else, and when they didn't, he began clearing the plates, leaving the forester gazing at those somehow familiar brown eyes and the lovely mouth curved in a slight and surprised smile.

He reclined on her couch watching one of his favorite old movies, *Casablanca*, with Humphrey Bogart and Ingrid Bergman. He'd loved the movie because of what it was, but also because Ingrid Bergman reminded him of his late wife. After she died, he tried watching it once, but looking at the similar features sent searing pain through his heart, and he hadn't tried to watch it since. This time, there was a gentler feeling of loss, but he could feel joy with that recognition. He could see bits of Christa in the actress's face too.

The dinner was far from what he was used to eating at the cabin. He cooked very simply for himself, and Christa's food was punctuated with color and herbs and spices in just the right blends to send his taste buds dancing all the way to dessert. "How do you keep your figure when you can cook like this? I don't want to stop eating!" He patted his full stomach and groaned a bit.

"I eat slowly. I really taste what I'm eating, and then I feel satisfied eating less," she nodded toward what had been her respectably filled plate. "That was just enough."

The forester remembered sitting with his dog at their special spot on the hill, overlooking the fields and mountains at sunset. Feeling every moment of that left him satisfied too. "Christa, you're a wise woman."

She burst into a delighted laugh. "It's just learning along the way."

They cleared the table together and he settled back on the couch, Christa beside him. Her voice came softly, "I want to thank you for asking me to the New Year's party, and for such a wonderful day today. It's been a long time since I enjoyed myself so much—not since Peter died. I smile, and I still do my best to enjoy every day as much as I can, but it's been so hard. . . ."

He felt deeply ashamed. He was so wrapped up in himself, in his own memories, that he had forgotten she was also suffering a loss, and one much more recent than his own. He felt a swell of admiration for the gentle strength she had that radiated all about her. Unlike him, she had been strong enough to accept the help and love of her son, whereas he had drawn away from his daughters, and so they had finally drawn away from him. He took her hand in his. "I would very much like to keep enjoying days with you." She sighed, and he continued. "I think you know I'm attracted to you. I think I knew I wanted to see you again the first day I met you in the forest."

"Me too, but I didn't know if I ever really would. I just hoped so."

He put his arm around her, and she nestled into his shoulder, the need for words gone for the moment.

Chapter Eleven

He felt awkward at the church. He didn't know the customs or the prayers and hymns. He felt as if everyone knew things he didn't, like there was some special code a person had to say to get to God, and he suddenly feared it was a code he didn't know and wasn't sure he could learn.

He never felt that way in the forest and fields. There, his heart ached with joy to be in the solitude of all creation, being accepted and just part of it. The code was written inside everything there, it seemed. There wasn't a chant. There wasn't a formula. It simply *was*, and it had filled him.

Here, in church, the opposite seemed true, and he felt empty and apart. The only ember of happiness was having Christa seated beside him when the pastor asked everyone to wish each other peace. Suddenly, strangers turned to him and shook his hand, some even leaving their pews to come meet him. He feared reaching out and feeling each grip and anything else it might bring, but every handshake was warm and welcoming and free of surprises. He forced the smile at first, and then gradually he felt a warmth and relaxation spread inside him as more and more hands gripped his and wished him peace. *Maybe if I think of them as trees. Like the king in David's story, we all are like trees, aren't we?* The idea helped. His smile became real.

"I see she got you to come! Saying no to her is hard, isn't it?" The forester turned to the familiar barking voice and saw Carlton towering as large as his tone and with the characteristic grin on his face.

"Carlton, hello!" The forester grimaced inside at the thought of a handshake, but Carlton solved the problem by slapping him soundly on the shoulder instead.

"I remember meeting you at the New Year's Eve Party! Had to leave early though. Wasn't feeling too good!" Carlton grinned in a way that would have made anyone doubt this man could feel anything but wonderful.

"I noticed that you left; are you feeling better, then?"

The forester didn't know if it was possible for Carlton to smile any wider, but he did, and his eyes twinkled brightly. "Oh, been better, I guess, but I can't complain! Be on the mend soon I'm sure!"

"Peace, Carlton."

"Peace, Michael!"

The pastor was a woman, which had completely surprised the forester. As the people were returning to their places for the rest of the service, he finally whispered this to Christa.

"Things change, don't they?" She winked then began to sing along with the closing hymn. He heard her voice, strong and clear, with the other voices. He was sure he could pick out Carlton's too, and he let himself sing along loudly, his bass blending in.

There was a church lunch afterwards, and Christa took him from small group to small group introducing him. He was surprised that a number of them had hiked some of the trails he maintained, and they remembered some of the special places he had created to rest or view natural wonders. These people weren't so very different from him. Maybe he wasn't so very different from them.

People there were from all walks of life and all ages. As usual, he ended up with a small group of children around him, and he was compelled to tell them stories. Christa threw him a knowing glance and continued visiting with some friends. He was just finishing one tale when Christa returned with a husband and wife in tow. "Michael, this is Jacob Newly and his wife, Margaret."

"Michael, so good to meet you."

"You have quite an amazing voice," his wife burst in.

Jacob laughed. "We direct the choir, and I have to ask if you'd consider joining. We don't have many strong basses."

The forester shook his head and looked away. "I don't know this music. . . ."

"You can learn it. Everything is new until any of us learn it," Margaret burst in again. She grinned sheepishly. "Sorry, I just get excited about music."

"Let's sing something we both know right now, shall we," Jacob said.

It took a few minutes to find a tune they both knew, but soon Jacob Newly and the forester were singing together, their voices ringing through the church basement. It brought the visiting to a respectful halt, and when they finished, the forester was mollified by the applause.

Carlton approached and stood before the forester silently for a moment. For the first time since they had met, the man's face was close to solemn. "I'm glad God let me live long enough to hear you sing!" The forester didn't know what to say; he'd received one of the most precious gifts one man could give to another, and he felt he really did love this man who was somehow so like a child.

Chapter Twelve

None of the three homes they toured spoke to him. Christa tried to be helpful, pointing out the pros and cons of each, but she finally admitted she didn't think any of them were a fit for him either, although she couldn't put her finger on why not. The closest to right was the cabin with the state land around it, but the cabin itself was small even by his standards. "Things always look much better in the pictures," he'd grumbled to her as they looked at a kitchen that both of them had a hard time standing in at the same time.

"That's good marketing," she reasoned, the businesswoman coming to the fore. "Those pictures at least got you here, didn't they?"

"False advertising," the forester continued to grouch.

"Like a woman in a push-up bra I suppose."

He guffawed, his grouchy mood shattered, but she kept looking through what little there was of the cabin with a no-nonsense air, as if she hadn't spoken anything surprising in the least.

The realtor promised that he had other properties he'd love to take them to see. Some were vacant, and he had free access to them as he needed, and he made some quick phone calls to arrange tours of two others. They all had a bit of land, but the forester was frustrated by what he'd known to begin with. He hadn't chosen these houses from the website descriptions because they were either too large or needed too much work. After spending most of the day looking at what he knew he didn't want, the forester politely told the real estate agent that he'd think about what he'd seen and get back to him.

"There's one more place I'd like to show you," the realtor pressed. When the forester started to wave the offer away, he said, "It's on the way back for you anyway. There's a side road off of this road that we'll need to take for only two miles out of your way. Just follow my car and pull over when I do."

They drove through rolling hills with open fields until they reached a side road on the left. It curved and brought them higher and higher until they reached wide fields at the top. In the distance was what looked like a sugarbush. The forester parked his car on the side of the gravel road, following the realtor's lead, and he and Christa got out, surveying the view. Christa's hand flew to her mouth. "This is just gorgeous!"

They could see for miles.

"Have you thought about building a place of your own?" The realtor handed them a paper with measurements, price and description. "The farmer who owned this is subdividing, and this is one of the prime lots. Ten acres, and can you *imagine* waking up to this view every morning?"

The forester looked at Christa and saw in her shining eyes that she was imagining it.

The realtor took advantage of his edge with her and moved towards her with an almost conspiratorial air. "I would face large windows toward that southerly view," he nearly whispered. "Maybe a deck too."

The forester looked at the beauty stretched out before him. It was covered with white now, but he knew how it would be in the spring. There would be green grass and buds on the trees. Birds would be singing and there was probably a fox den in one of the knolls where the vixen raised kits each year. He imagined cows grazing, and if they didn't graze anymore, then he could imagine the nesting field birds that would take advantage of the tall grasses to raise their own young. He felt a pang in his heart. "I can't build here. There's already too little land left. I'm not going to stick a building on this."

The realtor's face looked caved in then brightened. "But you realize if you don't, someone will anyway. No one is going to buy this choice property to leave it a field."

"Someone probably will build on it. It won't be me."

He saw mixed emotions on Christa's face and he didn't want to look. When they got back to the car, he tried to explain. "I used to get so excited about the idea of building my own place when I was younger, Christa. It was staking my claim—making my mark. My wife and I built our first house near the house where I grew up. It was a field too, flat though, but the area was still beautiful in its way. It still had quite a bit of land around it where I had played when I was a boy."

He breathed deeply, nearly going back to the place. "We chose a field with a forest line in back, and a giant rock. My wife loved the rock for some reason. There was plenty of room for our first daughter to play, and our second daughter loved the rock too. She'd climb it and stand on the top like a tiny queen."

"It sounds like a wonderful place to have started your family," Christa spoke softly.

"It was. What was the harm in building one house there? We loved it, and we were just one little family. Twenty years later, do you know what it looked like? It was a suburb—worse than that—there wasn't a spot without a house, and the traffic was constant. I'm told it's worse now. It isn't even safe for children to cross the road there. There aren't any wild animals except gray squirrels and some birds, and they only stay because people feed them. Everything else has been driven out. Anything that doesn't scavenge off our garbage has been driven out. The beauty has been swallowed whole."

"The Bible says man has dominion. . . .

"I don't think it means for us to swallow all of His other creations whole." He hadn't meant to snap it out, but she had to understand this. If she didn't understand . . .

"Christa, I'm sorry. I didn't mean to sound rude to you. I'd never ever want to be rude to you. This is a really important part of me. Do you understand?"

He held his breath as he looked from the road quickly to catch her eye.

"I do understand. I just hadn't thought about it this way. I've certainly noticed how places have built up, but . . . I suppose I've always thought like your real estate agent—'if you don't build there, somebody else will.'

They drove for the remainder of the ride in silence, but the forester felt it was the somber silence of Christa turning the new point of view around in her head and deciding what to do with it. When he brought her to her driveway, she put her hand on his arm. "How do you feel about building on a spot where there was something before—say a home that burned down."

"I could live with that. I just don't want to add to the sprawl. If there's already a foundation, and a well. . . .

"Then, are you in a hurry? Because I think you shouldn't drop me off yet. There's something I want to show you."

He could feel something swell up inside her like the excitement of watching a loved one unwrap a present. He felt it build in her throughout the drive as she told him where to turn. They were about five miles out of town in the opposite direction from the beautiful mountain-view lot when she told him they had arrived. She was almost bursting when they got out of the car. "I used to visit my best friend here when I was a girl. Her name was Rachel."

The forester looked at the property. There was no house and the snows covered wherever the foundation may have been. What he did see was a modest-sized barn set back from the road. There was what was once pasture on one side and behind the barn. On the other side there was a tree line. There was a certain wild beauty about the place. "I don't see a 'For Sale' sign here."

"The family hasn't listed it yet. I just happened to hear the other day that they had finally decided to do something about it. Rachel's children don't want to live here and Rachel already has a home." She pointed to the spot where they were parked. "This was the driveway. It goes back quite a way, and the house was across the drive from where you see the barn."

"Most farms I've seen were careful to build the barn further away from the house—I've always figured because of the smell," the forester mused.

"It was never a large working farm. Rachel's parents and her grandparents before them lived here and just kept animals for themselves."

"That explains why the barn isn't huge." The forester craned his head toward the building. "Do you think they'd mind if we walked over to see?"

"No! It's just an old barn. It can't even be locked, and they're like family to me."

They began trudging through the snow, the forester glad they had both thought to wear winter boots just in case they wanted to look at the outside of the homes they planned to see today. He felt he was on a mission, and when they reached the weathered boards, he pressed a hand against the wood. He nearly felt a pulse—a warm pulse. It felt like a solid old place, but it was lonely. It wanted filling. They moved to old double doors held closed by a large iron bolt. Christa slid it open and they tugged together at one side to pull the door open through the snow that drifted there.

Once inside, a surreal stillness enveloped them. It was a solid shell, amazingly straight, with nothing inside except wisps of hay from years ago and some metal parts that could have belonged to old haying equipment. They walked to the middle and stood there, surrounded by silence and history. "I like it." His voice finally cut through the air.

Christa walked to what looked like a small room in one corner. "This is where Sugar stayed. Sugar was Rachel's buckskin pony. She's buried somewhere on the property. . . . So you think you could build where the house was?"

The forester walked beside her and took her hand. "No."

"No! Oh, I thought you said you liked it."

"I do like it, but what we're standing in is what I see as the house. There could be a large kitchen over there that opens to a dining room, kind of in an open floor plan—then there's plenty of room for two reasonably sized bedrooms. It would all be one floor, which would be great considering I am getting older."

Christa's brown eyes widened as if seeing the place for the first time. "Now that's something I would have never thought of—making a barn into a house!" She folded her arms and looked around critically. "Of course you'd have to make sure you have a place where you can write."

The forester rolled his eyes with a chuckle. "Whatever you say."

When he returned to Don and Anne's house, he found some graph paper, a ruler and a pencil and began roughing out a floor plan. Don was still at work, and Anne breezed in with bags of groceries. Her eyebrows flew up when she heard what he was working on. "Michael, you're a terrible influence on my husband! He's going to love that, and then it's going to be weekends of driving around looking at vacant barns. This all seems like a good idea for you, but I will be damned if I'm going to live in a barn!" She set a package of chicken on the counter with a thud.

"Anne, I won't let him get carried away. He said he wanted to live vicariously through me, that's all."

She stopped in her tracks and turned to give the forester a hollow, hopeless stare. "You certainly know him well enough to know that's where it starts."

"I *promise* to do my very best to discourage him from getting carried away, Anne." She finished putting the groceries away, her mumbles of worry fading as she climbed the stairs.

He went back to planning, everything from where he could put a furnace or hot water tank to jotting notes on some things he'd like to build for the inside. He'd like to have a window seat where Christa could curl up and read. His pencil flew over the side of the paper to get a design down for the window seat before he forgot his vision.

As he was drawing, his mind suddenly snapped to Carlton's face and the appreciative, close to somber expression he had when he said, 'I'm glad God let me live long enough to hear you sing.' Suddenly, the forester was flooded with grief, and he pushed the paper aside and sobbed, glad that Anne had gone upstairs and didn't see the sudden change.

For the rest of the day and into the next, he could barely hold his composure. Every time he allowed thoughts of Carlton to slip into his mind, the great sorrow came over him and he would break down in tears. He stayed in the guest room as much as possible until Christa coaxed him to join her at church.

He tried to smile when all the newly made acquaintances welcomed him back, but he didn't know if he was able to hide how dead his eyes felt. There was a bar of iron around his heart, heavy and cold. As if in response, Christa was also quieter than usual. It was in this frame of mind they greeted the news together.

The pastor looked grim when she approached the front, bowing her head first then asking her congregation to pray for Carlton and his family. He had been diagnosed with inoperable cancer just days before. The forester clenched his fists to try holding in the pain, but the tears seeped out of his eyes although they were squeezed shut. Again, death! Why did he have to know? Why did he have to feel it? He felt the room spinning, but the pressure from Christa's arms around him made the spinning slow and finally stop. He felt something wet on his neck and realized she was crying too. "I have to go out! I have to leave," he whispered into her hair. The rending emotion was building inside, and he was using everything he had to control it. Once outside, he released the pain.

Christa smoothed his hair. "I had no idea he meant this much to you already."

"I don't know why he did, but he did." The forester took a handkerchief out of his pocket and wiped his eyes, trying to breathe more normally. "I knew."

"You knew what?"

"That he was going to die—that he was sick. I know this may be hard to believe, but I felt something the first night I met him—at the party. He shook my hand and I felt it." He couldn't take it back. He said it and it was out there. He didn't look at Christa, but waited for a long moment while there was only the sound of cars passing by, the tires crunching on the snow, and the sound of a hymn just beginning in honor of Carlton.

Finally, he couldn't stand it anymore. "You don't believe me, do you?"

"No, I believe you, but it's kind of *hard* to believe at the same time—I'm not saying you'd make up anything like that," she hurried, "but it's just . . . a bit shocking. How do you know you felt it? How do you know that's what it was?"

"Can we go to your place? I can't go back in there right now and if you want to know, I guess I can tell you, but not standing here. I've spent most of my life not wanting people to know and not even understanding it myself."

When they were settled on her couch, each with a cup of hot tea, he told her about his grandmother and his childhood experiences all coming back so vividly in the dreams and the severe depression that came over him before his wife's own diagnosis and the voices he heard that God was coming then.

She set her tea down slowly. "You heard voices? Did you hear voices with Carlton?"

He wasn't sure what her careful expression meant, and he started to seize up inside. "No. There weren't any voices—just pain and then horrible sadness."

"Michael, voices and visions—some of those things could be part of schizophrenia." When he pulled away from her touch, she reached for him and grabbed his hand. "I have to say it. Have you considered it? Have you told a doctor these things?"

He felt like he was sinking and suddenly alone again. He made one last attempt. "I don't believe these things are because I'm crazy."

"I'm not saying you're crazy—I have family with mental illness too, and it's amazing what medications can do to help."

"I'm not mentally ill," he looked imploringly, his hazel-green eyes reaching into hers.

"If what you say is true, that means that you're saying God has given you some kind of special power? Are you saying you have some direct line to God the rest of us don't have?"

He tried to speak, mouthing the words soundlessly at first then finally having them come out in a rasp. "I'm not anything special. I didn't ask for this and I don't know what I'm supposed to do with it. . . . I'm nothing special." He weakly waved his hands up and down his own body to show her.

He watched helplessly as tears filled her eyes. "Michael, I don't know what to think."

He rose and got ready to leave. There was no point in staying now. "Neither do I."

He drove from Christa's house, breathing deeply in and out, trying to calm the raging feelings for Carlton, and for the doubt he saw in the eyes of the woman he loved. He pushed that aside forcefully and focused on Carlton. They had driven by his house once, and he felt the need to go there.

When Carlton's wife opened the door, her face was strained, but she smiled gratefully when she saw the forester standing there. "Carlton will be so happy to see you."

He was reclining on the couch, with the familiar grin lighting up his face. "Michael! In quite a bit of pain today, so I didn't think it would be much use to sit on the church pews! They're hard as a rock you know!"

"I've only been there twice, but I do know," he forced a smile. "I'm so sorry to hear, Carlton." He put his hand out to his new friend and he gripped it back solidly. This time, he was surprised that he didn't feel anything but relief.

"Don't feel bad for me, Michael! I'm going home to the Lord! It's a time to rejoice, not cry—I'm ready! I'm glad God let me live long enough to meet you."

The forester was lifted by this man's never-ending pool of love and optimism. "I don't know if you'd like this, but suddenly a story came into my mind. Would you do me the honor of hearing it? It's meant for you."

Carlton grinned, and his eyes sparkled. "Let's hear it!"

A man was walking along a path. He was a big man, and sometimes he would speak too loudly or say things he didn't mean to say. Now along this path people were working in the fields. When they saw him coming, they would turn their backs on him or would stare but not speak a word to him.

Then one day the man was walking and an eagle attacked a small bird that, in its fright, flew into a branch and fell to the ground. The man stepped off the path and, standing over the small bird, scared the eagle off. He then reached down, pulled up some dead grass and putting it into one of his hands, made a tiny nest. With great gentleness, he picked up the bird and placed it in the nest in his other hand. Tenderly, with much care, the big man ran his finger over the body of the bird, felt the beat of its tiny heart, and knew it had life.

He then walked over to the tree and sat down beneath the branches. Raising his knee, he placed his hand with the tiny bird in its nest upon it and waited. The love and warmth from his heart went to his hand, warmed it, and from his hand to the nest, and from the nest to the bird.

In time, there was a stirring in his palm. The little head peeked out from the nest and looked about. Seeing no danger, there was a rustle of feathers, and the bird flew away. The big man smiled, arose, and continued on his way once more.

The people of the field had been watching him and had seen all of this, never before realizing his gentleness and the goodness of his heart. The next day

*when he appeared, walking along the path, they
stopped him, and were good to him, for now they truly
knew him."*

Carlton beamed. "That's me! That's me walking
down the Lord's path!"

The forester stayed awhile, listening to Carlton
and his wife talk about the past, and the diagnosis,
and what would happen next. They were so strong
that he had no choice but to draw some strength
from it too. When Carlton started to fade, the
forester hugged the large man and went away. As he
drove, he thought of one of the dreams he'd had
back in the cabin. The voice had said those innocent
and pure of heart have given the Lord what He's
asked for already, and that what seemed suffering to
others was borne by them with His grace. He
thought of the light in Carlton's eyes despite the
pain, and the grin he rarely went without. He also
thought of his own wife.

When she was in the hospital, she was still
attending to the needs of others, and never lost her
warm nature. He would visit her at the hospital and
find her consoling other patients or at the window of
the nursery, looking with a winsome smile at the
newborn babies. She had the same light in her eyes
that Carlton had now. It was love. He hadn't been

able to understand how it could be there, and he almost resented it at the time. How could she be so calm? How could she love seeing new life when hers was seeping away? That's what the light was—love, pure and simple. *She never went to church. She never opened the pages of a Bible, but somehow she gave God what He was asking for.* He thought it was amazing how it seemed so easy for her to do the right things. Toward the end he'd promised to be strong for her and to watch over their children, but when she had finally gone, he had surrendered to self-pity. He had to make sure not to make the same mistake again. He had to see the strength in these people and do things differently than he had then.

He knew what Carlton's future held, but he wasn't sure what would happen with his own.

Chapter 13

The only problem with using the barn as a skeleton for his future home was that it was only late January and not much could be done until the weather was warmer and the ground thawed. That meant he had to be without his dog even longer. He ached for the solace of the furry head. He wanted to lie on the floor and feel his friend's heartbeat near his own. If he'd bought a house outright, the paperwork would not only be started—as it was for the purchase of the barn and property now—but he would be moving in with his dog within a month. Still, this felt like the right thing to do.

It had been a week without a word from Christa. Of course Don and Anne both encouraged him to call her, but he couldn't do it. She thought he was mentally ill, and obviously didn't want him. His wife had accepted the things he told her so easily. Other than with his wife, Don, and of course, his grandmother, he hadn't felt accepted or safe to share the things he felt and saw with anyone. "And this is why," he murmured to himself.

What would his grandmother say if she could speak to him now? He thought of the beautiful vision of her holding out the steaming food on

Christmas Eve. If he trusted that, she seemed to be saying he was where he needed to be, that he would be nourished there—with those people—on this path. But he still didn't understand what the path was or how it could be right with a woman whose first thought was that he was mentally ill.

Carlton's wife had called days ago. "They think this is going to be fast, Michael. The cancer had already spread and is growing—we would both love to have that story you told. I don't want to impose, but could you write it out for us? Carlton has thought about it every day, and he wants to keep hearing it."

"I'll do anything you need," he told her.

He wrote the story with a pen and Anne typed it, printing it out on some paper with the image of a rainbow etched with misty softness on it, a barely powder blue covering the rest. It filled one page perfectly, and the forester chose an oak frame for it. It didn't seem like enough to do for a dying man and a grieving wife, but it was what he had to offer and it was what they wanted. He dropped it off that early evening, but Carlton was already so changed that he was too exhausted to visit more than a few minutes. Still, the amazing light stayed gleaming in his eyes. It was joy and love. So much joy and love.

The next day Don left for work, and Anne visited a friend. The forester paced the house and found it impossible to feel settled. He tried to read, but his mind wouldn't focus on the words. After scanning and rescanning the same sentence half a dozen times, he snapped the book shut and let it drop on the nightstand next to the living room chair. He looked around the house for something that might need fixing, but Don was obsessively on top of anything that might need repair. He stared out the window at snow falling down. It wasn't slow and meditative snow, but blowing at an angle with some rogue flakes spinning and twisting in their own directions. It would be cold, but he had to get out into the air. He threw on a wool jacket, a hat, and gloves and trudged the three miles to the café. When he walked through the door, his eyes fell on the table where he and Christa had breakfast together not long ago. He felt a hand squeeze his heart, but he took a deep breath and walked past the few customers to a small table in a corner.

"Michael!"

The forester turned sharply and saw a man just rising from a table in the café window. He wasn't very tall, but he reminded the forester of a proud and good-natured bantam rooster with his head high, posture perfect, and shoes flawlessly shined. The forester turned and walked towards the man, smiling, but mind madly seeking. *I know the face. I know the voice. Who? Where?* He took more steps and was nearly there. He imagined music playing, and voices singing in a choir, and it struck him soundly. "Jacob Newly!"

"Good to see you again! Please, please join me. I'm just having some coffee and a Danish. I had to get out of the shop for a while." Reading the forester's question, he added, "Margaret and I have a music store." The man nodded quickly as if his line of work would be no surprise, his full and cheerfully red cheeks bouncing a bit. "I was hoping you'd seriously consider what Margaret and I had said to you at church. We really would love to have you join the choir. Have you thought about it at all?"

The forester placed his order for just coffee with the waitress and shook his head. "I appreciate the offer, and I feel honored, but I can't see myself doing that right now."

"Well, I'm certainly not going to pressure you . . ." The man laughed and the red on his cheeks glowed even brighter, "but I will say that if you change your mind the offer stays. You really do have a wonderful voice. . ."

He cut his sentence short to stand again and wave to a woman walking down the sidewalk. When she didn't see him, he knocked on the glass and she jumped a bit, startled. The forester was surprised she could walk at all since she was so loaded down with books in her arms and a fully packed knapsack on her back. She was wearing a bright yellow jacket that somehow paled when her face lit up in a smile, revealing two of the biggest dimples the forester had ever seen. Her short hair peeked out from under a yellow hat, flipping stylishly against her cheeks as if to call attention to them. *What a cute little leprechaun! She must be Irish,* the forester mused. Jacob Newly hurried to the café door and flung it open for her when he saw her starting towards it. She barely made it through the door with her things, and she breathlessly accepted his help to set them on a chair at the table he and the forester were sharing.

"I heard you were back in town, Megan. Margaret told me you found yourself a little place on the lake."

"I've finally gotten settled in. Oh, what a job that was! I have to say I wasn't prepared for how hard it would be to leave a life I'd known for so long and try to fit the things that had so many memories from so many years into a little place somewhere else."

"I'm sorry, did your husband pass away?" the forester asked. The little leprechaun looked at him curiously.

"No, I just went through a divorce."

"Oh." The forester felt his cheeks flush.

"It's nothing, don't worry about it. I don't mean it's *nothing*. I'm not saying it wasn't horrible for a while, but I'm moving on."

"Are you always so loaded down?" The forester gestured to her things and grinned.

"I do a lot of different things to make ends meet, and it makes life easier if I have all my materials at hand."

Jacob Newly nodded quickly again. "She teaches French, does landscaping, and is a coordinator of a women's support program. Margaret also told me you're learning Russian and have taken up weaving."

The forester raised his eyebrows, a bit in awe. "I'm surprised you don't need a wheelbarrow instead of a knapsack to carry everything you need then."

"It could still happen." She flashed the dimples again and the forester heard himself nearly giggling. Jacob Newly introduced them. She chatted for just a while then slapped her hands on her thighs. "I'm tutoring a woman in French at the library next door.

I don't want to be late." She gathered her things, both the forester and Jacob standing to shake hands with her and say goodbye.

"It was good to meet you, Michael. Maybe we'll bump into each other again sometime."

He watched her hoist her knapsack, gather her books, and walk out the door and toward the library. "She's a survivor. Not afraid to tackle anything," he said to Jacob.

Jacob shook his head almost as if in disbelief. "That she is."

When he returned to Don and Anne's house, there was a piece of paper on the table with Anne's neat handwriting gliding over it. Christa called. Call back when you can. She popped her head through the living room door into the kitchen. "So you got the note?"

"Yes, I read it."

"Are you calling her back now?"

"I'll call her."

"Just let me know when you want to and I'll give you some privacy." Now she was standing in the doorway, looking at him, unblinking.

"I'll call her."

"Oh, I know. . . . Sooner might be better than later though, don't you think?"

The forester inwardly shook his head. He'd be lying if he said his heart hadn't leapt when he saw the words, but what was the point? What could Christa say? She'd already made it clear she didn't know what to think, and that what she did think was what he always feared people would think. *Not that I look down on people who are mentally ill, but that can't be it. My grandmother was different, but she wasn't mentally ill either; I would have known it.*

Or would he?

"Anne, you've known me for so many years—do you think it's possible that I'm mentally ill?"

She laughed at first then her smile faded when she saw his eyes. "No. I'll admit, I didn't understand your living in the forest all those years with hardly anyone to talk to, but Don said you seemed well, and that was enough for me. You're just—I don't know— a horse of a different color." She walked toward him and squeezed his arm. "Christa will come around. Maybe she has already, which is why you should call her."

When he did, she invited him to visit. "I want to talk to you face-to-face," she'd said.

The last thing he said to Anne before he drove off in her hybrid was, "I need to buy a car."

Chapter Fourteen

Christa had coffee ready when he arrived, but he waved it politely away. He'd had enough at the café. "I'll just have some water."

She led him to a small wooden table flanked with two overstuffed chairs. The one he chose had a forest green and burgundy woven blanket thrown gracefully over one arm. A large bookshelf engulfed the wall. He felt he'd stepped into an old English library. She carried a Bible with her and set it down on the inlaid wood patterned top. The forester couldn't help but lay his hand flat and smooth his palm and fingers over the table's finish.

"My husband bought this table for me after we'd taken a trip to Maine, and we stopped in an antique shop. I cried when I saw it. I don't know why, but sometimes beautiful things bring me to tears. We walked away from it and looked at all the other beautiful things, but I kept getting drawn back to this table, and when I touched it, I would find my eyes filled with tears. My husband said I obviously had to have it. He didn't understand why, but he didn't need to know why."

"He sounds like he was a good man. Like he loved you very much."

"That's all so true. He wasn't an artistic person. He was very down-to-earth and really wasn't moved to feel things strongly. He was the same most every day. Not high, not low, but so very even. He was my rock."

The forester felt her love for this man trembling inside her like a flower afraid to open. He knew the feeling, and reached across the table to touch her fingers. She hesitated, then turned her hand around so their palms touched and fingers entwined.

"You are nothing like him, Michael. I didn't mean to hurt you with what I said the last time I saw you, I just . . . I don't have experience with what you're describing. I talk to book companies, but not the authors. I admire the paintings, but don't know the artists. I was married to a wonderful man and I truly loved him, but he didn't have these *things*."

"I *was* hurt, Christa. I'm still hurt."

"I know. I'm trying to understand. It's just scary for me."

"So why did you call now?"

"I prayed. I asked for an answer, and I opened my Bible, and this is what I read: *Your young men shall see visions, and your old men shall dream dreams.* I took that as an answer, at least in part. I may not understand, but I should believe you."

"You said you're afraid, but now I'm afraid too. My wife accepted me with no proof. She didn't need any explanation. She believed in me without any hesitation at all."

"So we're both having to learn that neither of us will be a replacement for the ones we've lost."

"Yes."

"But maybe if we take our time, we can figure out how to be Michael and Christa. Maybe we were just so happy to have found each other we tried to move forward too fast. If we took things a little more slowly . . . would you be willing to try?"

He looked across the table. Her brown eyes were warm and hopeful, but there was the tinge of fear still there.

"I'd like that."

She smiled a tired but still radiant smile. "I'm so glad."

They fell into talking about the plans for the barn, and he shared that as much as he knew this was the right fit for him, he felt terribly lonely for his dog. When Christa asked why the dog wasn't able to stay with him at Don and Anne's, he explained that Anne had severe allergies to both dogs and cats. Christa brightened.

"I'm not allergic to dogs. We always had dogs, but our last one, Scout, died a year before my husband passed away. For some reason we waited to adopt another one, and then when I was alone, I just never did. I've been feeling very lonely for that friendship lately though. Why don't you have your dog stay with me? I'd be happy to have him, and that way you could have him close by—spend time with him—take him for walks when you want to."

The forester thought back to the time he tried to visit his dog where he was staying now. It seemed like a good idea. The dog turned and turned in ecstatic circles; they had a delicious long walk together, the dog pushing his nose in the snow and snorting, tail fanning with pleasure. Then it was time to leave, and the forester thought his heart would break when the dog tried to leave with him and couldn't. He watched the dog's joy collapse. Would it be different if the dog were here?

It was closer. He would be visiting more often, and his smells would be around the house at least in part. His dog also wouldn't be sharing time with four other dogs. He would be the center of Christa's attention when she was home with him, he was sure of that. So it was decided. "If you really think that would work for you, I'd like to take you up on it."

Christa glanced around the house with her eyes bright. He imagined she was picturing the house filled with the dog's love. "Well, then why don't you give them a call? We can go get him now as far as I'm concerned. We just need to stop at the store on the way and pick up some dog food and anything else he needs."

The forester felt a rush of joy sweep through him. "He has his collar, and a leash, and bowls. I think food is all we'd need to get."

"We'll take my car so Anne's doesn't get full of dog hair."

When they arrived to get the dog, he flew into circles again, sniffed Christa thoroughly, and jumped into her car and instantly flopped down as if they would need a crowbar to remove him. *I am NOT going back there*, he seemed to say.

"It's okay Buddy. You're not going back. You'll be staying with me for a while."

The forester smiled inwardly. She understood 'dog.' That was a good sign.

"I'm glad you named him Buddy. It really is what he means to you, isn't it?"

The forester looked back, the dog's mouth nearly splitting the shaggy face with a wide, toothy grin, the tongue lolling ridiculously to one side. "Words can't describe it, but I guess it's close," he mused.

The next Sunday, the forester and Christa planned to attend church and have a brunch afterwards. Buddy was settled into her house as if he'd always been there. She insisted on buying a special dog bed for one corner, but to her chagrin he wouldn't use it. Instead, she said he slept on the floor in her bedroom, much as he had with the forester at the cabin.

"He's used to the floor, and he has a lot of hair. That bed may just be too warm for him and too different," he told her.

He thought of that as they sat in a middle pew of the church, hearing the pianist play while waiting for Pastor to come to the front. Margaret Newly sang a lilting, soprano solo then the small choir backed her up. The forester closed his eyes to soak in the beautiful sound, and when he opened them, he saw Megan.

Chapter Fifteen

Megan's back was to them, so he assumed she didn't know he was there. If she hadn't just turned her face toward a woman who was talking to her quietly, he wouldn't have known she was there either. There was no bright yellow jacket, books, or loaded knapsack to have given him a clue, and he and Christa had arrived a bit late, slipping quietly into their seats.

The choir finished the last song, the notes still somehow humming in the air like a meaningful memory. Pastor walked to the front and the effect was ended, like her moving robe parted the sea of sound and made the vibration silent. She stood, facing the congregation, and the forester stiffened at her expression. He knew before she spoke.

"Some of you already know that our Lord and Savior has taken Carlton home." She announced the services, asked for volunteers to help arrange a church meal afterwards, and said there was a sign-up sheet at the kitchen door for anyone who would like to make the family a dish during this difficult time.

"You didn't know?" The forester whispered to Christa.

She shook her head. "I knew it was going to be soon, but I hadn't heard—I can't believe I hadn't heard. I would have told you if I had, Michael."

The pastor read a bit of scripture, and then looked down at some paper in front of her, a bittersweet smile crossing her lips. "There is one special reading I'd like to do today. It was at the request of Carlton's family, and I have to say that it gives me great joy to share it."

She paused and put her hand to her heart, closing her eyes and raising her head slightly to the sky, then opening her eyes again and letting them fall on the page. When she began to read, the forester's blood froze. It was his story—the one he had written for Carlton. First he was cold, and then he felt a flood of heat. Christa hadn't heard the story, but must have somehow recognized the tone; she looked enquiringly at him, but he was so overwhelmed he couldn't look back at her. The congregation was silent, listening to his words—the words from his heart about Carlton. He felt exposed, but a small light inside him glowed brightly. He could feel the people around thinking of Carlton in a different way. He somehow knew many of them were picturing themselves as the people in the fields who didn't see past the loud voice and the sometimes poorly chosen words. He heard a woman start to weep softly, and then some sniffles as people cried more quietly still. *But it's nothing really* a part of him argued. *It's just a few simple words from my heart.*

At the end, Pastor looked out at him and smiled. "Thank you for writing that, Michael."

Christa beamed at him. "I knew it."

At the end of the service, people came to the forester to shake his hand, to embrace him, and to tell him how much the story moved them. "I've told him he should write children's stories," Christa agreed.

"Oh, Michael, you should!" Megan had worked her way through the small group and took his hand. "Jacob and Margaret didn't tell me how much talent you have!"

"I didn't know about the writing or I would have. All I knew was the man can sing," Jacob tossed his hands in the air.

"Oh, that's wonderful!" Megan's dimples nearly winked. "Do you read music?"

"No. When I was in school they tried to teach us, but I could never get the hang of it." He was having trouble not thinking of Carlton. He was surprised that he only felt that calm sense of relief he'd experienced when he saw Carlton right after he was diagnosed. There was no pain anymore where he was.

"I'll bet you'd play beautifully by ear though. . . . I started playing the dulcimer when I traveled to Virginia a few years ago, and I meet with a few people in Derby once a week to practice. We're getting together tomorrow and it would be terrific if you'd join us. It's not a complicated instrument. I think you'll pick right up on it."

The forester grimaced. "I don't own a dulcimer to use, though."

Megan waved his hesitation away. "I have three of them. I'll bring the one I preferred playing before I got my new one."

"Try it, Michael," Jacob patted his arm. "Maybe if you like it you'll think again about being part of the choir. Music is like an addiction to most of us, you know. Once it's in your blood, you have to feed the craving."

Christa gave him a small smile. "It sounds like they really want you to go. Who knows? Maybe you can put some of that writing to music too." She smiled a bit broader and reached her hand out to Megan. "I'm Christa Thomas."

Megan took her hand and gave her the suddenly aware, curious look she had given the forester in the café when they met. "Megan Donnely. Do you sing or play?"

Christa pursed her lips and shook her head. "I sing here, but I don't have any talent to speak of, and I never played an instrument."

"Not even in school?"

"No. I was too busy reading."

Megan flashed her dimples again. "Well, there's no harm in that! Some people are just . . . *specialists* I guess. I just can't be content with any one thing. I have to do everything I can. It seems there's not enough time in a day to do and learn all the fascinating things that are out there."

Megan led the forester into a building shaped like an octagon. There was a terra-cotta surface covering it that flowed as smoothly as marzipan frosting draped over a cake. He touched it with his fingertips. "What is this?"

"It's a straw bale structure," Megan said. "What you're touching is concrete stucco. I helped build one of these when I was in New Mexico."

"You certainly have traveled!"

"I go where my interests lead me. I lived there while I worked on my Ph.D. in Theology."

"And you happened to build a straw bale house in your free time?"

She laughed. "I told you, I feel like life is short. I want to do everything. I want to learn everything."

They opened what looked like a handmade dark-stained wooden door that was almost medieval with heavy black wrought-iron touches and walked into the small space. It was cozy thanks to a small soapstone wood stove on one end, flames dancing in the glass-windowed door. Otherwise, there was little else except chairs and floor cushions, some simple music stands, and white walls. Three others were already there, picking at their instruments or unpacking them, chatting pleasantly.

One of them, a small blonde woman, looked familiar and the forester squinted, trying to place her. She raised her eyes and met his. "You don't remember me, do you?" When he couldn't give a quick answer, she stood up and shook his hand. "Stephanie. I was one of the nurses at the hospital with your wife in those last two weeks before she went home for hospice. We all loved her—she was such a special person. I was going through some difficult times then, and do you know that despite her own pain she was the one who helped me? I'll never forget the nights she had me sit next to her bed and talk with her. She had so much to share. What a wise and gentle woman."

The forester suddenly remembered walking into his wife's room and seeing the little blonde nurse there, sitting in the chair beside the hospital bed and leaning forward as if drinking in every word. His eyes misted with joy. "I do remember you."

"And who would have thought that all these years later you'd be here in my home learning to play the dulcimer!"

Megan handed the forester a case and lifted one of her own. He opened it and looked at the strange instrument inside. One more person arrived and Stephanie showed the Forester briefly how to hold it and generally how to play. While she greeted others and passed around a plate of vegetables and dip, the forester sat with the dulcimer, picking at the strings and listening to the sounds. Two of the others were warming up and playing what they called "old mountain tunes" he didn't know. He watched for a while and then thought of a song he'd loved in his youth. He let the sounds fill his mind and move down his arms into his fingers then began to experiment with the strings, quickly getting the tune to sing from them.

"Oh!" Stephanie said. "You've played before. Megan thought you hadn't."

"He told me he hadn't." Megan knitted her brow.

The forester couldn't stop his fingers from playing now. He felt the vibration of the music work its way through him and started softly singing the words despite himself. He thought he'd forgotten them, but there they were—only hidden and not lost after all. When he finished, he sighed as if something heavy had just been lifted away. "I haven't played before."

Megan looked ruefully at her own instrument. "It took me two years of practice before I could play like that. You're a natural!"

He continued to meet with the group, and Megan, once a week. Megan let him take her dulcimer home so he could practice, and he spent a good deal of time playing it for Don and Anne and for Christa. The feeling of relief he felt after playing it relaxed him more than he had been since he left the cabin and his forest. Christa asked him to play for her when she was cooking dinner, or when she had paperwork to catch up on for her son's business. Buddy would lay nearby with his head on his paws, looking up at him as if sharing the forester's mood.

"I think it's time to give Megan her dulcimer back and get one of my own," he set the instrument down and walked to the stove where Christa was cooking, sampling a bite with a fork that she handed him as if on cue.

"I think you should. I'll bet they have them in that music shop in New Hampshire that I was telling you about. Maybe we could go next weekend and look."

The forester just finished chewing the sample with reverence. "Actually, Megan is taking me to a place just across the border in Canada. She said they specialize in tribal and rural instruments there."

"Oh." Christa gently tossed the pan's contents. "You're spending a lot of time with Megan."

"She's a fascinating person. I've never known anyone like her."

Christa flushed. "She certainly is adorable too." Buddy stood by, waiting hopefully, and she threw him a piece of cooked chicken. "So did you find out when the crew is coming to start on the barn?"

The forester moved behind her and gently put his arms around her waist, leaning his head forward and resting his face in her silken copper hair. He breathed in, smelling the soft scent of her and let his lips touch the tresses. "They'll start this Monday. Before you know it, I'll be picking out furniture and moving in."

"Are the girls still coming to see it?"

"Last I knew Taryn is, but Sonya wasn't sure if she could afford the flight. I offered to pay, but you know how all of you modern women are. You think you have to be completely independent."

"Well, in the case of your daughters, I'd say the apples fell right next to the old tree!" She shot him a playful look.

"Are you saying I'm old?"

"No. I'm saying you've been one of the most independent and solitary men anyone could know—at least until recently."

"Ah, yes." He nodded sagely. "But I learned to accept help when I needed it. Sonya hasn't learned that lesson yet."

"Maybe I could talk to her." Christa turned off the burners and crossed the room to the phone. "What's the number?"

She dialed and began an instant flow of conversation that lasted for over twenty minutes and resulted in Sonya agreeing to have her father help with the plane ticket if need be. He was blissful listening to Christa's voice rise and fall, and the intermittent silences as she listened to his daughter.

Chapter Sixteen

It was years since the forester had spent time alone with either of his daughters, and he reveled in how familiar yet odd it seemed to walk with Taryn down the driveway to the barn that was soon to become his retirement home. He brought out the floor plans he had designed himself and led her inside, showing her each area, walking from place to place as if the walls were already there. The sounds of pounding hammers and electric tools filled the air, and Taryn inhaled the smell of cut wood.

He'd had to choose some newer lumber, but he'd spent extra to get as much reclaimed wood as possible from a mill that specialized in that a few towns away. "I'm spending your inheritance," he laughed as he showed her the pile that they had delivered.

She huffed. "You know Sonya and I don't care about that. It's great to see you happy. Live your life, Dad. Don't worry about us."

"Your mother raised you right."

"I think you had something to do with it too." She rested her head on his shoulder and looked around at the chaos. "Dad, it's going to be amazing. I can't wait until Sonya sees it."

They went to the café for lunch afterwards and talked about the past and the things that Taryn and her husband were planning to do with their own home. Perhaps because of her work with children, she had sudden and whimsical urges to use rooms of their home like a canvas, and she gestured passionately as she described her latest vision of an Egyptian-themed basement. "The other day I just saw it—walls painted like faux stone blocks and Egyptian touches everywhere."

The forester shook his head. She'd always had fits of fancy, and luckily for her, she had married a man whose happiness largely depended on helping her make those visions come true. "I think you're like your great-grandmother," he told her. "You just do what you're inspired to do and you don't question it, even if it doesn't make sense to anyone else."

"Well, then I'm like my father too. I think losing the business was one of the best things that happened to you, Dad. After that, you started doing things you needed to do instead of what the world expected you to do—and yes—even when it didn't make sense even to us."

She had just finished speaking when Megan burst through the café door, loaded down as always with the pack, but her arms were free. "No books today?" The forester called to her and her face lit up.

"No. Everything fit in the bag today." She turned her Irish charm towards Taryn. "You must be Michael's oldest daughter? I'm so happy to meet you! Your father is such a talented musician that I'm jealous; did you know how good he is?"

Taryn sipped some water with lemon and shrugged. "I grew up hearing him sing, but we never had instruments in the house."

"Well, you *have* to have him play for you while you're visiting. He's amazing." She turned to the forester again and laid her hand on his. "When we go to pick out your dulcimer, do you want to drive or should I? Either way, I thought you might like to meet me at my place and have some lunch before we go."

They quickly worked out the details and Megan hurried back out toward the library, which seemed to be her own private classroom. When the forester looked at Taryn, she was leaning back in her chair a bit, arms crossed over her chest, eyeing him appraisingly. "How does Christa feel about that?"

He returned to eating his cooling food. "About what?"

"About this Megan chasing after you?"

The forester felt something strange inside that he couldn't name, and he found himself waving his hands and blustering, "Really, Taryn! She's a friend. She's not interested in me as anything more than that. What would make you think anything else? She came in and spoke to us for all of five minutes. The poor woman. . . ."

Taryn raised both her hands and closed her eyes. "Stop. Don't say another word and let's see if I get this right. The poor woman is alone for whatever reason, right? Maybe a divorce. She seems ultra independent, and she doesn't have much—she says she doesn't need much, right?" The forester started to speak again, but she crisscrossed her hands to have him wait. "She isn't what she seems, Dad. She's a survivor, I'm sure of it, and while that's not a bad thing overall, she's seeing you as her ticket to surviving in the future. She's like a stray cat that thinks she's seen a nice warm house to live in."

"That's not a nice way to describe her." The forester was gripped with annoyance and tried to let his eyes burn that message to his daughter, but she either didn't see or wasn't put off by it in the least.

"I'm not saying she's a bad person, but she wants you for what she thinks you can offer her in the way of security she's lost, and she isn't the kind who cares that you're seeing another woman. She'll manipulate her way in until she either upsets Christa so she leaves you on her own or until she gets you, she hopes, to weaken."

The forester was slow to anger, but he felt his cheeks burning and his muscles tightening. For a moment, he was nothing more than the father of a naughty child, and his voice deepened as he leaned towards her, his hazel eyes staring unblinkingly into hers. "I want you to stop right now. You don't know her. You don't know a thing about my relationship with Christa, and perhaps you don't know me after all."

Her eyes flashed with pain for a moment, but she breathed in resolutely and softened her own tone to meet his. "Dad, you aren't the only one who knows things sometimes. I've realized a lot about myself in these last few years. I've noticed that I always seemed to know the right person to befriend and whom I should avoid. I never dated any guys who really weren't nice, did I? At least, not after going against my instincts once and learning. Do you remember the plane trip we took to the Midwest when I was five?"

The forester felt his anger ease just a bit as the image of his five-year-old daughter flashed into his mind. Her sister wasn't even born yet, and they were waiting at the airport to check their baggage. Little Taryn was casually strolling close by and looking up into the faces of other travelers, smiling, when suddenly she'd run back to her parents with terror on her face. "You said there was a man there who scared you, but when we asked you to point him out, you said he was gone."

Taryn nodded. "He was standing there waving to me to come over to him and smiling, but his smile seemed more like a grimace to me than a real smile. It was too eager. When I was five, though, I didn't have the words to explain that to you and Mom. A couple of years ago that memory came back to me as clearly as if I were there. I shut my eyes and tried to remember exactly what had terrified me so much, and I *did* remember now that I had the knowledge and words to describe it. He wanted to snatch me, Dad. I didn't know what that was at the time, but without knowing, I still knew that this man wanted to take me and harm me, and I even had some sense of sexuality with it. I didn't have any experience with sexuality, but there was this sense of it all around him."

"You could have had those memories develop from the news and from your experience over time, don't you think?"

"Think about it, Dad. Think about me. Was I ever afraid of people? Ever?"

Despite himself, he felt his face break into a broad grin thinking of her fearlessly approaching complete strangers and starting spirited conversations as if they had been great friends for years. They had had to be careful with her because of that. One day there had been a man walking down the road with a dog by their home. Taryn was playing in the front yard and it was a weekend, so he was actually home, replacing a loose brick on the front steps so no one would get hurt. He had his back to her, and didn't see what was going on until her high voice rang out with joy, chattering away like a squirrel.

When he turned, he saw a tall, shirtless man with long, matted hair and an also long and scraggly beard walking down the road, his daughter of only four gamely prancing along beside him and asking him where he was from and where was he going? What was the name of his dog, could she pet him? The man's pants were dirty, and the dog was thin. Not starved, but certainly as lean as his companion. He had called Taryn back sharply and gave her a very serious warning about talking to strangers, but she had only looked at him as if he was speaking another language and never did stop her overly friendly behavior.

He reminded her of the incident and she smiled. "I wasn't afraid of people who didn't mean any harm. That man looked a certain way, but how people look doesn't fool me. I feel them instead of see them sometimes. The man in the airport was very clean-cut. I can see him in my mind even now. He had dark hair parted on the side in a bit of a cowlick, and he wore clothes that looked a bit like business clothes. He was very put together, but that's not what I felt from him. He looked good, but wasn't."

"You feel everyone?"

"No, not everyone. Most people just slide by me because I think there isn't anything strong to feel one way or another, but once in a while it's overpowering."

"It's a bit like me." The forester felt suddenly shy. He hadn't discussed much of his past with either of his daughters because it somehow seemed wrong to burden them with it. A thought struck him. "How did you know that I 'know things sometimes'?"

"Mom told us."

The forester felt like someone had thrown him a fastball that he wasn't ready to catch. "I had no idea she'd done that."

"She wanted us to know before she died. She said you'd be in a very bad way when she was gone, and asked us to be patient with you and to understand that if you disappeared into yourself, it wasn't that you didn't love us. She wanted us to understand that this has always been very draining and difficult for you."

"Did you tell her about your own . . . thing?"

"I wish I had, but I couldn't. I didn't realize it myself until just those few years ago. Somehow, I think she knows, though."

They sat silently together for a long time, slowly eating, the forester thinking about all that they had just shared. Finally, he looked up at Taryn. "Your great-grandmother said she had a purpose with what she called her gift. She said she grew things. That was it. She grew things. Do you know what your purpose is?"

Taryn nodded and smiled a bit sadly. "I help people along."

"Along to what?"

"Wherever it is certain people need to move along to. I don't usually know where I'm helping them to; I just do as I'm inspired and the answer comes when they've arrived. Sometimes it's to a realization. Sometimes it's to an opportunity. Sometimes it's to let go and die in peace."

The forester's eyes misted and he pursed his lips to control the sudden emotion. "That's what your great-grandmother said. She just did what she was told." A glimmer lit in his heart. "Christa said something similar."

"Christa is a deep and wonderful woman, Dad. I know Megan is fascinating, and she's sweeping you up into music and it seems beautiful, but *be careful*. That's all I ask of you. You would ask the same of me if you felt you had to." The waiter brought the bill and she brushed away the forester's attempt to pay. "My treat, Dad. What's your purpose?"

"Isn't it sad," the forester grimaced and shook his head. "I'm in my sixties and I still haven't figured it out."

"You're fighting it for some reason. Why?"

"I don't know."

"Maybe it's harder for a man to let go of control. You really have to do that for it to work."

Taryn hugged him and kissed his cheek before hopping into her rental car and heading to the next town to visit an old school chum. He watched her disappear and walked slowly to his own car, unlocked it, and sat inside, surrounded by silence and lost in his own thoughts.

Chapter Seventeen

The forester went to bed that night and wasn't surprised to find himself standing in a room with beautiful music playing. There were three ministers sitting at a card table. The tune wasn't anything he recognized, but it filled his mind until he forgot that this was only a dream. All he heard were the strains of sound massaging his brain and pulling him towards the table. The ministers kept playing cards as if he wasn't there, the black and red faces flipping outward at intervals in some kind of matching game he didn't know but wanted to learn. He watched their moves carefully, trying to see the pattern, but each of them seemed to be playing by different rules. Still, they smiled and laughed and flipped the cards as if it was completely intentional. A voice began to sing, and soon the forester realized the words were about his other dreams and his visions. It sang about the ball of light, and when it did, one of the ministers suddenly looked up and gazed deeply in the forester's eyes gasping, "It's like Moses!"

The forester started backing away when another minister patted the air serenely with his hand and said to his cohort, "We can all be Moses if we play our cards. These are the cards he needs." The forester saw a close-up of the calm minister's hand reaching to the deck. He lifted it up and his voice was gentle but strong: "Choose your cards."

The calm minister held the cards out even closer to him. "Choose your cards."

The forester pulled one, and then another, then looked to the minister to see how many he was to take. The minister smiled. "You'll know when you're through."

He began pulling cards again, and suddenly there were no more although the deck had seemed much bigger. When he counted his cards, the forester saw he had seven. "What do I do with them?"

"Look at the hand you've been dealt and play it. Please, pull up a chair." The minister gestured to an empty seat, so the forester pulled it up to the table and fanned his cards to see what he'd been dealt. All he saw was a red, swirled design on the backs. He was sure he had taken the cards in the proper direction, but there was nothing to see. All the ministers had now stopped playing and were looking at the cards he held, nodding, and then returning to slapping their choices down on the table. "Everyone else sees your hand," the calm minister told him. "You need to play them so you can see."

The forester felt panicked. "How can I play if I don't know what I'm laying down? You all seem to know the rules, but no one has taught me what to do."

The minister's tone was unchanged. "You've been taught this game since childhood, but you haven't really joined in. Play a card."

The forester took a card and turned it, but all he saw on the other side was more of the red, swirled design. He turned it and turned it and started to feel cold with fear. The minister laid his hand on the forester's. "Play a card."

He slowly reached his hand close to the table's surface and laid the one card on top of another a minister just set there. When he looked at it again, he saw the word "seven" written on it. The others had numbers, but his had the number written out. The calm minister broke into a suddenly wide smile. "Good! You tell a marvelous story!"

Every time the forester laid down a card, the number or image was written as a word. All the ministers continued laying their own cards down, and the forester felt filled with joy.

When he woke, he was very hungry and thought he would love nothing more than to have breakfast with Christa. He was picking up Sonya at the airport later, and the next day he would be going with Megan to buy a dulcimer. He thought of Taryn's warning. *She could be right, but there's a chance she isn't,* he mused silently. He would be careful.

Christa seemed especially willing to eat out, and she suggested trying a little diner closer to where his new home would be rather than going to the café. "Just to try something different," she said brightly.

The place was small, and one woman worked behind the counter cooking where all the customers could see. She took the orders, cooked, served, and cashed people out with a rhythm that was nearly impossible. "I never thought watching someone do this kind of work would be beautiful," he whispered to Christa, although he knew that as close as the quarters were, the woman could probably hear anyway. He hoped he was offered some privacy from the sizzling of the bacon on the griddle.

"I know! She's doing three things at once and still managing to be polite and carry on conversations with people. This is her thing I guess." They watched someone else's breakfast get served while theirs was in process, then they watched the woman start another four eggs for some new people who had just placed an order. Christa shook her head with admiration then turned her attention to her date. "Michael, I want to talk to you about Carlton's story."

He nodded for her to go on.

"I did something with it, but I didn't ask you first. I'm sorry about that—but I really think it needed to be done."

"You burned it?" The forester chuckled and she gave him a soft, joking slap on the upper arm.

"No. I sent it in to one of the publishers we distribute for."

The woman behind the counter had set juice in front of them and he'd just been drinking it. He nearly spit it back out. "What? Christa, that was something I wrote for Carlton. That wasn't meant for anyone else. I don't even know how I feel about having it read in church." He squirmed in his seat.

"It's simple, but it's a great children's story. This company publishes Christian children's books." When he grimaced, she continued. "You don't give yourself enough credit. Michael, your stories have a clean and simple wisdom to them. They move adults, but they're simple enough for children to understand and love. It just seems obvious to me that you have a gift, and it also seems to me that it's a crime to waste it."

"Or maybe a sin?" He managed to smirk wryly. "It's just that I can't imagine they'd want anything of mine. That story didn't take any time. It came out of nowhere and I wrote it down. I haven't had any training and haven't spent blood, sweat, and tears on writing like writers seem to always have to do."

"Maybe when it's the right path, it isn't hard to walk it." Christa took his hand. She lowered her voice. "Maybe you're inspired to share these. You told me your grandmother had visions of some kind too, and that she was the first one to tell you it was a gift. What did she do with her inspiration?"

The forester looked at the plate just set before him. There were potatoes with onions, eggs, and whole wheat toast. A cluster of grapes garnished the side, and he picked them up, turning the cluster about and inspecting the red, round fruit. He suddenly imagined all the things on his plate as they were once, growing in fertile soil somewhere, being tended in some way, seeded, grown, then harvested and now here to nourish him. He smiled a slow, deep smile of intense realization. "She grew things."

Christa was the first person he'd ever known not to ask, "That's all?" Instead, her brown eyes glowed with more warmth than he thought possible.

They ate breakfast and went back to Christa's house to get the dog. They decided to go together to pick Sonja up from the airport, and Buddy loved to ride. Since Sonya loved dogs, there would be no argument about sharing the back seat with a ball of love and hair. The forester told Christa about his grandmother's house, and the way it stood out of the barren urban setting like a real Garden of Eden. He described all the details he could remember of her working in the soil and carefully pruning away dead leaves and branches so others could have a better chance to survive. She created a compost of the pigeon droppings and food scraps and garden refuse and made sure the earth was ready before she placed any seeds there. There wasn't a thing she couldn't grow.

When he finished telling a beautiful batch of tales about her, Christa looked at him quizzically. "What do you suppose would have happened if you hadn't spent all the time you did at your grandmother's house?"

He thought of his parents—his father so much older than his mother, and prone to jealousy, physical fights, and too much drink. "I remember getting up in the morning and sometimes having to pick my mother off the kitchen floor," he sighed. "If I hadn't had my grandmother, I can't imagine what would have become of me."

"So she grew you too."

"Yes. She told me as much once."

When they picked Sonya up, she yelped with joy to see Buddy's hair flying in the back and wrapped him in her arms with almost more enthusiasm than she'd shown when greeting her father and Christa. "A little wild child," the forester explained. "She was the one always bringing kittens and stray dogs home. She found a toad once and kept it in a child's plastic swimming pool. I don't know how she did it, but it would eat ants right off of her finger."

Sonya finished kissing the dog's head and turned her attention back to the humans. "Oh, and don't forget the snake I used to wear around my neck."

"Oh, NO!" Christa shuddered.

"That's what most people said, but I never understood it." Sonya shrugged.

"I'm surprised you don't work with animals instead of children," Christa said.

"I work with children *and* I teach them about animals," Sonya patted Christa's arm. "Don't worry; if they are afraid of snakes, I don't force them to be too close."

They reached the driveway of the barn and took Sonya in. Taryn was waiting inside. There was an amazing change from when he had been there the day before, and he stood with his daughters and a wonderful woman beside him, sharing it like a family. It seemed as though everything was developing before his eyes.

Chapter Eighteen

Christa snuggled in the crook of the forester's left arm. His dog lay curled on the right side, head on his friend's lap. "I don't know if it's a good idea that we let him on your couch like this," he murmured into her hair.

"They don't live as long as we do, and I don't mind giving him some comfort while he's around. So what if I have hair on my couch? It cleans."

The three of them rested there awhile, floating in a state of bliss the forester knew all too well should be grabbed onto and held—savored—because moments like this were the things worth remembering. They were the things to call forth when times were not so good. "When my wife died, I wasn't able to think of the good times to see me through," he kissed Christa's temple. "I won't make the same mistake again."

She turned her head to look into his eyes, a smile creeping on her lips. "So are you expecting me to be gone soon too, Michael? I don't think you're going to have any such luck."

"I'm not saying that, but you never know what unexpected things happen."

She frowned a bit, and shifted, causing the dog to raise his head too. "But you said you wouldn't make the same mistake again, and there you go. This is a perfect moment and you're bringing sadness in before anything sad has even happened."

"I promise I'm not. I'm reminding myself how wonderful this is. I'm feeling nothing but joy and contentment. I'm taking stock of it."

"Logging it in your forester's notebook?" She laughed softly.

"Logging it forever. Keeping it so I can pull it out when I need it. I'm actually aware of this moment now—I'm totally here—like I almost never was for my wife. I loved her so much, Christa, but I was always somewhere else. I was in the past, or in the future, or thinking about business, and I never realized what I was missing. Now I have a second chance to really do it right."

"You're going to really live!" Christa pumped her arm, hand in a fist.

"I think I am."

She pulled away from him and the dog jumped suddenly from the couch. "You're going to make your life matter!"

"I think I am!" He smothered a laugh and sat up straight.

"You're going to listen to your heart and do what is in there from now on!"

"I suppose I really have to."

"You're going to write!"

The forester had his mouth partially open, ready to agree to the words she was to say next, heard them, and gaped. He put his hands to his face. "Not this again."

"Come with me, Michael! Tell me the story about the man over the hill. Let's write it down." She took his hand and tugged him. *She's glowing like a young girl,* he thought. He felt strangely young too as he looked at her flushed cheeks and sparkling eyes. Her bangs had fallen a bit over one eye, and she hurriedly brushed them away. He couldn't resist the tug anymore and rose to follow her, smiling but complaining all the way to her study.

"I don't know which story you mean. I'm not a writer, Christa, I keep telling you that."

"Remember July Fourth? You told the story to that beautiful dark-haired little boy about the old man that the children called 'over the hill,' and when he went 'over the hill,' it was a beautiful, magical place full of wisdom and vision—and *dragons.*"

The forester squinted, trying to remember. He did somewhat, but like an echo in the mountains or a movement caught out of the corner of his eye.

"When I tell stories, they're a bit like dreams. I tell them, but then afterwards I can't really remember them."

"Like those perfect moments you used to have but didn't bother to log in your 'forester's notebook'? Well, maybe that's why you should write them down. Come on, I'll tell you what I remember and it might help you fill in the rest."

Christa pulled out a laptop and described what she recalled to the forester. He listened and was surprised that it did seem to return to him. He told her the words, his eyes shining now, lost in the imagery in his mind. She was there next to him, her fingers flying over the keyboard, but somehow he was transported to that other place. He saw the old man, not so unlike him, but not him, and the boys in the field playing a game of ball. He saw their faces with a lack of respect because there was so much they still didn't know. He walked the meandering path up the hill, the colors growing more vibrant with each mile, and finally reaching the beautiful zenith and the valley on the other side—over the hill—where dragons flew and he was invited to see so much from astride the back of the gold and blue dragon; he felt the scaly nub the old man held onto as the dragon flew. He nearly tasted the air, sweet with the essence of fruit trees below. He felt a rush of happiness when he spoke the dragon's answer to the old man's question of why he hadn't been here before now: *You were not yet over the hill.*

When he was able to focus on Christa again, she was smiling, with tears misting her eyes. "Now, *that's* your gift, Michael. Your grandmother grew things. Taryn helps people along, and you tell stories."

"I tell stories. . . ." He tried the words on to see how they fit. They did. He thought of the dream he had with the ministers and how words had appeared on the cards instead of numbers. The main minister said he was quite a storyteller. How could he have missed it for so long?

Christa explained some things about children's books and took some out to show him. Together, they spent the evening breaking the words into the right number of pages, making sure one page left the young readers wanting to turn to the next to learn more. It fell fairly naturally into the format, and Christa shook her head, bemused. "You were right about the whole thing being too easy for you. Some people take a year or more to hone their story and this just falls into place. May I send it out for you?"

He looked at the pages she held, set up like a book and waiting for paintings to fill the white space along with his words. It was his first story written with his acceptance. *I tell stories.* He felt a tingling sense of completion, like a puzzle piece that had been missing had been found, finally locked in its rightful place. How had he lived without that feeling for so long?

The forester's fingers strummed over the dulcimer at the store while Megan and a salesman looked on. There were many sizes and slightly varied shapes, all having their own particular feel and sound. He tried several, but this one was feeling most promising. It made his muscles relax like they were melting from his bones. "I think this one chooses me," he handed the instrument to the young man with multi-colored hair and wasn't surprised when he didn't have to feel strangely about making it sound like the instrument somehow had a voice in its partner.

The young man nodded and smiled, lifting the dulcimer and giving it a loving gaze. "You made a very good choice. I'm partial to this one myself."

"It is beautiful, Michael." Megan put her arm around the forester and lay her head on his shoulder for a moment, then snapped her dimples toward him merrily. "Now you have your own. We should celebrate! When we go back across the border, I want you to have dinner with me at my place."

"Oh, you don't have to do that."

"Don't be silly! This is an occasion, and I had it all set up before we left. Everything is chopped and ready to go; all I need to do is put it on the stove when we get there. It's called *Chicken Trieste*. It's one of the best meals I make, and I'm making it for you tonight." She lapsed into an Italian accent, making the forester laugh out loud. She learned how to make it, of course, when she traveled with her husband some years ago in Italy.

"I haven't mentioned anything to Don and Anne about not joining them later."

"I already told them I was surprising you, so no worries there."

The U.S. border wasn't far from the store, and they crossed without incident, driving another half hour to her tiny lakeside home. "Bring the dulcimer in with you. Maybe we'll play together for a while after dinner."

Once inside, she handed him a glass of red wine and put on some classical music, lighting a series of candles on a table already beautifully set, and more candles arranged all about. The dining room, living room, and kitchen were small and open to each other—one basic space. There was one bedroom and a bathroom upstairs over the open floor plan downstairs. "It's small, but it's what I can afford right now," she had explained when he first had visited there. "At least I'm by the water."

Tonight they talked about music and writing while she stirred garlic and green peppers, sautéing them with delicate chunks of chicken, then squeezing a bit of fresh lemon over the pan. She dipped her finger against the lemon she had just squeezed and ever so slowly stroked her wrists and the spots just below her ears as if putting on a rare and priceless perfume. "Mmmmmm—I love fresh lemon. It's so light and makes me feel like I'm in the Mediterranean. Have you ever walked through citrus groves, Michael? The orange and lemon trees in the hot sun make the air smell like citrus. It's absolutely intoxicating." She laughed and added cream to the pan, heating and then thickening it.

"I haven't in reality, but in a story I just wrote, I could have sworn I did—riding on the back of a dragon and smelling the fruit from the trees even up there in the air."

Megan drained noodles, put some on plates then ladled a healthy portion of the Chicken Trieste over the top. She grated fresh cheese then placed her plate on the table, and the other in front of the forester. Her wrist and arm passed closely to his face, and he smelled the lemon, now blended softly with the heat of her skin. She drew her arm slowly away and seemed to drift to her chair. "I'm constantly amazed by you, Michael. I've never known anyone like you." The forester had trouble not looking into her eyes as she folded her hands together and rested her chin on them, elbows on the table, gazing at him and smiling slightly.

"Believe me, I'm just like everyone else." He dipped his fork into the noodles and sauce, bringing the first bite to his mouth. "Megan! This is delicious."

"Oh, you're not like everyone else, Michael. I've traveled plenty and have met a lot of men, and I think you're very special. You play music with so much passion. It takes you like a lover."

The forester felt heat rush through his body. "I do love to play, and it relaxes me, but I'm sure you've known other men—and women— who get lost in the music."

"I suppose I have known a lot of passionate people, but trust me, there's something special about you."

They ate the rest of the meal, Megan refilling the forester's wine glass once and sliding her fingers along his back before returning to her chair. The heat inside him was growing, and he noticed things about her he hadn't before. He saw the way her lips moved when she ate, and he suddenly imagined kissing them.

"Oh, I'd better stop eating or I won't be able to play with you."

The forester pushed his empty plate away a bit and stood quickly. "I really should go."

Megan stood quickly too and hurried to his side. "But we haven't broken in the new dulcimer yet! That's the whole point of tonight, isn't it? Please stay, Michael. Stay and play with me." She leaned up against his body and tilted her mouth towards his. He felt glued to the spot although his brain was telling him, in some far-way and muffled voice that he should leave now. "You don't have to leave now." She pressed her lips to him, and he found himself tentatively pressing back. "You don't have to leave tonight at all."

He shook his befuddled head and pushed her weakly away. "Megan, I'm with Christa. This isn't right."

"She isn't even an artist, is she? She can't understand you the same way you and I could understand each other."

"I love her. I do feel like we understand each other."

Megan's dimples all but disappeared in a flash. "You're making a mistake being with her. Anyway, I don't see a ring on your finger! You can still make another choice."

Suddenly, the fog in the forester's brain was gone, and he looked at Megan as if he was outside of himself. She helped him see something he should have realized before.

He stood back from her, his eyes resting on his left hand. "You're right."

Chapter Nineteen

That weekend the forester knew he had to tell Christa what he had done. He was ready, though. It was strange how he really didn't question his decision at all. It had all become clear at that moment, that evening, in Megan's lakeside home. He had always been so busy fighting the things he was told to do that the messages through the years had only seemed garbled in his mind, but if he had done as his grandmother had told him and just listened, they really were plain and simple.

He cleared his mind and allowed himself to know what to do next. He had the sudden image of the old oak tree and his bench in the forest. It was the place where he first saw Christa and where he first knew he might want to date her, hold her. It seemed logical then that it was a good place to have the dating end. Everything then would come full circle.

Anne brought a wicker basket and handed it to him wordlessly, then grabbed him in a tight squeeze. Finally, she pulled back and whispered, "I hope it goes well."

He winked. I know you're worried, but I'm not. This is the right thing and I know it will turn out for the best."

"I know it's the right thing, but I feel nervous for you. Can't I just feel nervous for you?"

He smiled. "You can feel whatever you want for me, as if I could do anything about it."

His hands, already so much less calloused than they were five months ago, folded a piece of paper and put it in an envelope. It wasn't a story this time, but certainly a way of using his words to explain to Christa as best he could.

The forester walked along the path that was so familiar, and his dog bounded by his side, tail waving with approval. The only difference now was Christa hiked along beside him. They were quiet most of the way, the chorus of spring birds filling the trees, and squirrels fresh from their winter naps scurrying about through the leaves. Trees were well budded and Christa exclaimed in delight when they reached the oak and bench and found the trilliums blooming not far from the base. "Oh, Michael! Look at them!" She stroked their deep purple petals and carefully touched the elegant green leaves. She turned her eyes to the oak stump, setting her hand on the moss-covered bark. "Imagine what she saw in her lifetime."

"She? I always thought of this old timer as a 'he.'"

"Maybe the tree reflects whatever the onlooker is."

Michael smiled at the tree, and the smile reached far past his face. He felt it unfurl in his stomach and spread like the dead tree's branches once reached, with large limbs, then smaller offshoots, and smaller ones, creating a never-ending web of joy in every part of him, body and soul. He unpacked the wicker basket, handing Christa a beautiful crystal glass Anne had loaned him from her collection. He took one too and lifted a bottle of wine, uncorked it, and poured them each a small glass. The finishing touch was a picnic of homemade bread, a selection of meats and cheeses, and the red grapes he loved so much. He could feel his grandmother nearby, relieved and happy for him.

"I want to make a toast," Michael began, "with some words I wrote for you."

Christa clapped her hands together once and gripped her fingers together playfully. "You wrote me something?"

"I did. But this is *not* for any publication. It is for you. It's between you and me, okay?"

She rolled her eyes not unlike the first day he saw her with her son, and he could still hear her correct herself from calling her son Mikey. "I think we could negotiate some kind of deal."

He pulled the folded piece of paper out of the basket and looked across into her brown eyes, so much like a doe, trusting and lovely.

If love is the shine of her auburn hair,
If love is the glow of her skin so fair,
If love is the curve of her precious nose,
Lips full and red as petals of a rose,
If love is the brown in her beautiful eyes,
Then at last I know where my captured heart lies.
If love is the voice of a babbling brook,
And the sweetness of lovebirds in lingering song,
Then love is a gift and a delicate thing
That can humble a great man or powerful king.
. . . And to this love I give a gift. . . .
MY HEART.

He reached into his pocket and pulled out a case, opening it, revealing a ring set with seven small diamonds. He kneeled at the base of the bench near Christa's feet. She looked back at him with so much love in her eyes he thought God had never made a more beautiful creature than this woman he hoped would agree to be his wife for the rest of their days. "Will you, Christa Thomas, be by my side as I want to be by yours?"

Her hands flew to her mouth and she reached down to him to raise him up and pull him beside her on the bench. "How long do I have to wait?"

After they ate, they stood before the remnants of the oak tree and looked at it a long while, arms around each other. "There's one more thing I'd like to do before we leave here," Michael said as he pulled his old worn Bible from the basket. He reached for Christa's hand and laid it on the cover, placing his own gently over hers. "Let's open it together and see what it has to tell us."

Together, they let the pages separate, and Christa let her finger fall to a section. They read the words together. *I am pressed, but not broken. I am confused, but not despairing. I am hunted by the enemy but not abandoned by God. I have been thrown down, but I am not finished yet.*

Michael sighed, waving his arm and hand over where the top of the tree once would have been. "Can you see how it once was and how it will be again?"

Christa rested her head on his shoulder, pointing to the young oak growing below. "I can."

*. . . your young men shall
see visions and
your old men shall
dream dreams.*

— Acts 2:17